06-01

Newbery girls

⇥ Newbery Girls ⇤

❧ *Newbery Girls* ❧

SELECTIONS FROM FIFTEEN NEWBERY AWARD-WINNING BOOKS
CHOSEN ESPECIALLY FOR GIRLS BY HEATHER DIETZ

With an Introduction by Barbara Elleman

MARGARET K. McELDERRY BOOKS
New York   London   Toronto   Sydney   Singapore

Margaret K. McElderry Books
An imprint of Simon & Schuster Children's Publishing Division
1230 Avenue of the Americas
New York, New York 10020

The Newbery name and medal are trademarks of the American Library Association and are awarded
through the Association for Library Service to Children.
A portion of the proceeds from *Newbery Girls* will go to the American Library Association.

Table of Contents

⟿ *Introduction* ⟾

Have you ever met Claudia, the main character in *From the Mixed-Up Files of Mrs. Basil E. Frankweiler*? She runs away with her brother and hides out in the Metropolitan Museum of Art, where the two eventually solve a mystery about an ancient art object and make friends with an eccentric old woman.

Another character you're sure to like is the wooden carved doll in *Hitty: Her First Hundred Years.* Her amazing escapades are traced over a century of adventures. From her early beginnings with a sea captain's daughter to her life with a Quaker family, Hitty's life is never dull.

And then there is the title character in *Yolonda's Genius.* Big, strong for her age, and afraid of no one, Yolonda is determined to prove that her younger brother is a true musical genius. The chance to attend the annual blues festival in Chicago allows those plans to possibly come true, and Yolonda marshals all her resources to complete her mission.

Although these characters inhabit far different worlds and appear in books by different authors, they have one thing in common. All are featured in Newbery Medal or Newbery Honor books. Newbery titles all sport bright gold (for a Medal book) or silver (for an Honor book) stickers on their covers, immediately alerting you to a book of distinction. Given since 1922 by the American Library Association, the Newbery Medal recognizes one author each year for a distinguished contribution to children's literature. The story of how this award came about is a fascinating one, with some far-reaching connections. The idea for the award was conceived by a man named Frederick Melcher, who was not a librarian or a teacher, but a book publisher. While attending an American Library

Association conference in Swampscott, Massachusetts, in 1921, Melcher's ideas about the award came in a sudden rush of inspiration. His choice for the name was an Englishman named John Newbery, who had lived more than two hundred years before Melcher. In 1744, the thirty-one-year-old Mr. Newbery had started a bookshop in St. Paul's churchyard in London and hung out a sign reading JUVENILE LIBRARY. Melcher thought there could be no better way to honor the early bookseller who had first seen the possibilities of publishing books aimed particularly at children than to name a children's literature award after him. As more and more books for children were being released at that time, the librarians meeting that day in Massachusetts agreed an award was needed and thought that Newbery was a highly appropriate choice. Melcher engaged the sculptor René Paul Chambellan to design a medal, and to this day, a reproduction featuring his design is given annually to each winner.

When the first Newbery Medal was awarded in 1922, librarians across the country were invited to send in nominations, resulting in the participation of 212 librarians. Their overwhelming choice (163 votes) was *The Story of Mankind* by Hendrik Willem Van Loon. Today, a fifteen-member committee of librarians chooses the Newbery Medal and Honor books.

The eager anticipation concerning that 1922 winner is repeated to this day. Late in January of each year, the announcement of the Newbery Medal and Honor books is made on television, reported in newspapers, and posted in local libraries and bookstores. Often becoming instant best-sellers, the winners can be found in libraries and bookstores, stay indefinitely in print, and eventually join the realm of classic titles not to be missed.

In the following pages, you will find a wide-ranging collection of excerpts from past Newbery books, packaged to give you an opportunity to meet some courageous, fun-loving, innovative heroines. Although these are faces from fiction, you will undoubtedly find them inspiring and worthy as role models. Some of the selections go back to the early decades of the Newbery Medal, when sensitivities about race, gender, and ethnic backgrounds were different than today. Even so, the authors' words have been honored; no updating or editing has changed the original text. These books, after all, were written by authors who have made characters dance off the pages and into readers' hearts. Whether it's Claudia, Hitty, Yolonda, or other characters from books distinguished by a Newbery Medal or Newbery Honor, these heroines seem to call out, "Join our adventures!" Take their invitation; you won't be disappointed.

BARBARA ELLEMAN

REFERENCES

Fenner, Carol. *Yolonda's Genius*. Margaret K. McElderry Books, 1995.

Field, Rachel. *Hitty: Her First Hundred Years*. Macmillan, 1929.

Konigsburg, E. L. *From the Mixed-Up Files of Mrs. Basil E. Frankweiler*. Atheneum, 1967.

Smith, Irene. *A History of the Newbery and Caldecott Medals*. Viking, 1957.

Hitty: Her First Hundred Years

Rachel Field

—•: NEWBERY MEDAL, 1930 :•—

HITTY IS A SMALL WOODEN DOLL CARVED OUT OF MAINE MOUNTAIN ASH (FOR GOOD LUCK) BY A PEDDLER AND GIVEN TO THE YOUNG DAUGHTER OF A NEW ENGLAND SEA CAPTAIN.

IN WHICH I BEGIN MY MEMOIRS

The antique shop is very still now. Theobold and I have it all to ourselves, for the cuckoo clock was sold day before yesterday and Theobold has been so industrious of late there are no more mice to venture out from behind the woodwork. Theobold is the shop cat—the only thing in it that is not for sale, which has made him rather overbearing at times. Not that I wish to be critical of him. We all have our little infirmities and if it had not been for his I might not now be writing my memoirs. Still, infirmities are one thing, and claws are another, as I have reason to know.

Theobold is not exactly a bad cat, but he is far from considerate.

Besides, he is prowlishly inclined and he has the most powerful claws and tail I have ever known. Then, just lately he has taken to sleeping in the shop window with his head on the tray of antique jewelry. If Miss Hunter could have seen how narrowly he missed swallowing one of the garnet earrings when he yawned right before last, she would be very uneasy indeed. But Miss Hunter has had Theobold ever since she opened the antique shop and she seems to set great store by him for his trying ways. Miss Hunter has a good many queer ones of her own and I must say that I felt a little *wadgetty,* as Phoebe Preble's mother used to say, at first over her habit of poking and peering and turning everything upside down. One grows used to this in time, although it wasn't what I was brought up to consider the best manners. But Miss Hunter means well and if she decides you are genuine there is nothing she will not do for you. That is why after she found me knocked off my chair and on my nose three different mornings she said she would run no chances with such a valuable old doll but would take me out of the window each night before shutting up shop.

So here I am in the midst of her very untidy desk with my feet on a spattered square of green blotting paper, my back against a pewter inkstand, and a perfect snow bank of bills and papers heaped about me. Nearby, weighing down another pile of scribbled sheets, is an old conch shell. I have seen far handsomer ones in my time; still, it is a reminder. I cannot see the light shine on its curving sides without thinking of the Island in the South Seas and all the adventures that befell us there. Across the store on the mantelpiece is the model of a sailing vessel, square-rigged, in a glass bottle. But its sails are not so well trimmed, and its gliding not so fine as the *Diana-Kate*'s when we sailed out of Boston Harbor. Perhaps tonight the old Swiss music box will begin to play all of itself, as it does sometimes without the least warning. It is strange to sit here and listen while it tinkles out the "Roses and Mignonette" waltz with the same precise gaiety as in the days when Isabella Van Rensselauer and the rest danced to that tune at Monsieur Pettoe's select salon for young ladies and gentlemen. That was just across Washington

Square, scarcely a block away from where I sit today, but there were no skyscrapers then nor any street of little shops like this.

It may have been the ship in the bottle, or it may have been the music box, though I think it more likely that the quill pen gave me the idea of writing the story of my life. The pen belongs with the pewter inkstand, but quills are as much out of fashion today as whalebones in ladies' dresses and poke bonnets for little girls. Still, one cannot forget one's early training, and not for nothing did I watch Clarissa copy all those mottoes into her exercise book with a quill pen. If it is true, as Miss Hunter and the Old Gentleman declare, that I am the most genuine article in the shop, why should I not prefer quills to these new-fangled fountain pens? Nor am I inclined to scratchy steel affairs with sharp points. So I will be true to my quill pen which I now take in hand to begin my memoirs.

As far as I can learn, I must have been made something over a hundred years ago in the State of Maine in the dead of winter. Naturally I remember nothing of this, but I have heard the story told so often by one or another of the Preble family that at times it seems I, also, must have looked on as the Old Peddler carved me out of his piece of mountain-ash wood. It was a small piece, which accounts for my being slightly undersized even for a doll, and he treasured it greatly, for he had brought it across the sea from Ireland. A piece of mountain-ash wood is a good thing to keep close at hand, for it brings luck besides having power against witchcraft and evil. That was the reason he had carried this about in the bottom of his pack ever since he had started peddling. Mostly he did his best business from May to November when roads were open and the weather not too cold for farmers' wives and daughters to stand on their doorsteps as he spread out his wares. But that year he tramped farther north than he had ever been before. Snow caught him on a road between the sea and a rough, woody country. The wind blew such a gale it heaped great drifts across the road in no time and he was forced to come knocking at the kitchen door of the Preble House, where he had seen a light.

Mrs. Preble always said she didn't know how she and Phoebe would have got along without the Old Peddler, for it took all three of them, besides Andy the chore-boy, to keep the fires going and to water and feed the horse, the cow, and the chickens in the barn. Even when the weather cleared, the roads were impassable for many days and all vessels stormbound in Portland Harbor. So the Peddler decided to stay on and help with odd jobs round the place till spring, since Captain Preble was off on his ship for months to come.

At that time, Phoebe Preble was a little girl of seven with gay and friendly ways and fair hair that hung in smooth, round curls on either side of her face. It was for her that I was transformed from a piece of mountain-ash wood only six and a half inches high, nor nearly so tall as a bayberry candle, into a doll of parts. My first memories, therefore, are of a square pleasant room with brown beams and a great fireplace like a square cave, where flames licked enormous logs of wood and an old black kettle hung from an iron crane. The first words I ever heard were Phoebe's as she called to her mother and Andy: "See, now the doll has a face!" They came over to peer at me as the Old Peddler held me between his thumb and forefinger, turning me this way and that in the firelight so my paint would dry. I can remember Phoebe's excitement over my features and her mother's amazement that the old man had been able to give such a small bit of wood a real nose and even a pleasant expression. Surely no one, they all agreed, had so much skill with a jackknife. That night I was left to dry on the mantelpiece with the light from the dwindling fire making strange shadows, with mice squeaking and scampering in and out of the walls, and the wind outside blowing through the branches of a great pine tree with the sound that I was to know so well later on.

Phoebe's mother had decided that I was not to be played with until properly clothed. Phoebe was not a child who took readily to sewing, but her mother was firm, so presently out came needles and thread, thimbles and piece-bag, and I was being measured for my first outfit. It was to be of buff calico strewn with small red flowers, and I thought it was very fine indeed. Phoebe's stitches were not always of the finest. She was apt to grow fidgety after ten or fifteen minutes of sewing; still, she was so anxious to play with me that she quite surprised us all by her diligence. I do not remember exactly how I came by my name. At first, I was christened Mehitabel, but Phoebe was far too impatient to use so many syllables, and presently I had become Hitty to the whole household. Indeed, it was at Mrs. Preble's suggestion that these five letters were worked carefully in little red cross-stitch characters upon my chemise.

"But nothing is ever going to happen to her, Mother!" cried the little girl, "because she will always be my doll."

How strange it seems to remember those words now! How little we thought then of all that was so soon to befall us!

In Which I Travel—by Land and Sea

And so it came to be September, with such a shine on sea and leaf and every grass blade that even I experienced a strange springing feeling down to my very pegs. Never since then have I heard crickets make such high and persistent chirpings. All day and all night you might hear them at it in the brown, burnt grass.

"They're singin' to keep the cold away," Andy told Phoebe one night as we three sat on the doorstep, watching the big red fall moon rise behind the seaward islands.

"And can they?" Phoebe was always very curious about such things.

"No," Andy assured her, "they only think they can. The colder it turns the louder they holler, but the frost always gets 'em. You wait an' see."

"I'm glad we're not crickets," said Phoebe, hugging me tighter, as if she feared I might turn into one.

That night after the whole house was still and everyone in bed, I lay in my cradle and listened to them and thought of what Andy had said. I, too, felt very glad I was not a cricket.

Captain Preble was forever riding over to Portland to see if the post that came by stage three times a week from Boston had brought him news of the *Diana*. There had been many delays about the ship's outfitting and the Captain was growing impatient.

"Reuben Somes is first-rate at strikin' whales," I heard him tell his wife one day, "but he's no hand at gettin' a ship overhauled. Guess I'll have to go up to Boston by the next stagecoach if we expect to weigh anchor before November. This is the last time I put in at Boston. It'll be Portland for me from now on."

"Now, Dan'l, don't you go off 'fore I get your twelfth pair o' socks knitted," his wife begged. "I couldn't rest easy here at home if I thought you was sloshin' round in wet feet!"

"Guess there's nothin' for it but to fetch you along to Boston with me day after tomorrow," he laughed. "You can finish 'em on the way and fit yourself an' Phoebe out with new winter woolens in style."

"My goodness, Dan'l, who ever heard of such nonsense!" she answered with a serious head shake. "You always were one for extravagance—two lamps burnin' an' no ship at sea!"

Her words puzzled me at the time, but I later learned that this was a phrase often used by wives of whalers and meant that some one was spending what he had not yet earned. I was to hear many such sea terms before very long.

Somehow or other the Captain always got his way. So it came about that one fine fall morning we all set off to catch the Boston stage. The sun had been up only a little while as we went clattering away, leaving the square white Preble house, the red barn, and the ancestral pine behind us. Little did I think as these familiar shapes slipped from view that I was not to see them again in another week. No, not one of us guessed, then, all that lay before us as we turned into the Portland road.

Such a morning as it was, too! I shall never forget the scarlet of the swamp maples by every pond or bit of marshy land, the bright yellow of elms and birches, and the flaming red of woodbine that made the fences look as if they had burst into flame. It was golden-rod and asters all the way to Portland.

"There, Kate," said the Captain, suddenly pointing with his whip, "that's the first mountain-ash tree I've seen this fall."

There, sure enough, at the edge of some woods was a slim, tallish tree loaded down with bunches of orange berries. The tree seemed to bend under their weight and they shone like burnished balls.

"That's Hitty's tree," cried Phoebe, "and it's magic!"

"Hush, child," reproved her mother, "you musn't say such things."

"But the Old Peddler said so, Mother," Phoebe insisted. "Don't you remember when he was making her he said it was a charm against evil?"

"Well, now, I guess he was just givin' you a fish story," put in the Captain hastily, for he saw his wife look rather stern. "Anyhow, it's what I call a pretty sigh. Geddap, Charlie, or we'll be too late for the stage."

We were in plenty of time, however. In fact, the Prebles were able to stop for doughnuts, gingerbread, and glasses of cider at Cousin Robinson's on Congress Street where Charlie and the gig were to be left while we were away.

There are no such stagecoaches nowadays, or such fine, prancing horses to draw them. This one was painted red and yellow, and the four horses were matched in pairs, two grays and two chestnuts. The spokes of the wheels were painted black and when they turned very fast it made one quite dizzy, especially if one hung out of the window and looked down. Perhaps this was the matter with Phoebe, for after we had been jolting and rumbling along for about an hour she complained of not feeling well. Captain Preble and Andy had climbed up on top with several other men and boys and the driver. However, there were two or three ladies riding inside with us and they were full of sympathy and advice. One brought out peppermint lozenges, another lemon drops, and I think there were other remedies in the shape of dried licorice roots and homemade spruce beer. Phoebe tried them all. But none made her feel any better. She grew very pale and was glad to lie still with closed eyes as we rolled along at a fine pace.

"I am afraid," her mother told the other ladies with a doleful head shake, "that she must have inherited a weak stomach. It runs in our family."

I was happy to think that I was subject to no such discomfort. Though, of course, I had been unable to indulge in the cider and gingerbread at Cousin Robinson's! I suppose that may have had something to do with it.

We stayed the night at a fine old tavern in Portsmouth and were off again before daylight. Fresh horses were harnessed and the stage was soon rumbling toward Salem.

Phoebe proved herself a better traveler the second day, and her mother chatted with two new lady passengers, her needles clicking briskly as she continued to knit the Captain's socks. So past harbors and headfields, by farms and fields and elm-shaded village streets we came at last to Salem. Here was a fine harbor full of ships and larger houses than I had ever seen before. We walked up and down in the early twilight. Some of the houses were of brick with small square balconies built on their roofs about the chimneys. "Captain's walks," Phoebe's father said they were called, because one could walk there and see what vessels were in the harbor. Her mother kept marveling at the size and grandeur of the homes we passed, admiring the elaborate carving over doors and windows and the handsome furnishings that we caught glimpses of within.

"They can afford it," her husband explained. "Salem's 'bout the richest port there is in these parts. If I was to take you down to the wharves, you'd see 'em loaded down with cargoes from India and China and heaven knows where. Maybe if I strike luck this voyage and bring back six or seven hundred barrels of sperm [whale], we can come an' live here, too. How'd you like that, Kate?"

But his wife shook her head.

"You know well enough I wouldn't live anywhere except in the State of Maine. But I s'pose there's no harm in my admirin' other folks' front doors and parlor curtains, is there?"

The Captain allowed there wasn't.

By the next evening we were settled in Boston in a couple of rooms an old lady let out to sailors' families. The Captain had known her since he was a boy, and she welcomed us warmly. From her upper windows we could see the harbor with a perfect forest of masts where the vessels lay anchored near the wharves.

The Captain had gone at once to his ship, taking Andy with him. Phoebe and I were through supper and in bed by the time he returned. He sounded worried and kept repeating over and over that he should have come before and how they must get off soon if they were to make headway against the autumn gales. Some of his best men were sick or had signed up for other ships; the vessel was only half fitted out and he could not find a proper cook. This last difficulty seemed to worry him most of all. Ship's cooks were apparently scarce that year.

Several more days passed. The Captain was busier than ever down at the wharves. I had a feeling that something was going to happen, so I was not surprised when he came back one night and had a long talk with Phoebe's mother. I could not hear much of what they said, for Phoebe and I were in bed and they sat with their heads close together by the little glass lamp on the table. Captain Preble had charts spread out before him, besides a great many other papers, and his wife listened to him so intently as he talked and pointed things out to her with his big forefinger that she let her knitting lie idle in her lap.

"Well, Dan'l," she said at last, "I'll take the night to think it over and let you know by morning. I never 'lotted on going to sea, least of all to cook for a parcel of hungry men in one of these greasy old 'blubber-hunters,' as you call 'em."

"'T won't be so bad's you think," he told her, "there ain't another vessel has had so good an overhauling. You can fix your cabin up 'most as nice as if you was at home, and as for the work, why you'll have some one to do for you hand an' foot."

"But when I think of my kitchen at home," she sighed, "an' all my jelly there on the table, and our cow with the neighbors, and Charlie eatin' his head off with oats in Portland, I don't hardly feel I can."

"Don't you mind about that," he assured her.

"Well, if I do go the name of that ship's got to be changed to something more Christian." She spoke very firmly.

"They say it's bad luck to change a vessel's name," the Captain told her. "Not that I hold on to that sort o' thing, but crews get notions and you have to humor 'em."

But his wife held firmly to her convictions.

"Crew or no crew," said she, "I don't set foot on any ship with such a heathen-sounding name."

So the Captain said he would see what could be done, and by breakfast time the next morning it was all settled that we should go.

Phoebe and I spent most of the day by ourselves, for the Captain and his wife were both far too busy making last purchases and seeing to all the final preparations on the eve of our departure. We were glad enough when Andy put in his appearance after supper to help a couple of big sailors carry down boxes. Andy acted very important and proud of himself in the new pea-jacket and sea boots that Captain Preble had bought him. He seemed years older than he had a week before and took his new duties as cabin-boy very seriously. I did not think he sounded particularly pleased to have us going along.

"They all say a vessel's no place for women folks," he explained to us, "and they don't want you to go only for the pie and doughnuts."

"Well, I don't care what they say," Phoebe told him with an emphatic shake of her curls, "we're going. Father said so this morning and he's Captain."

It was well after sunset by the time we went down to the wharves, but we could make out the dark outlines of hulls and masts and the shapes of men and piled-up cargoes in the flickering light of lanterns and the thin fall dusk.

"There she is," said the Captain suddenly, pointing to a looming shape alongside of the wharf. "That's your new home, Phoebe. Reckon you're goin' to like it?"

We were swung aboard like so many parcels. High overhead the masthead lantern gleamed whitely in a circle of paler light it sent out into the darkness. Below us, strapped into a little sling of a seat, a man was whistling as he moved a big brush to and fro.

Captain Preble beckoned us over to watch him.

"There's Jim," he said to his wife, "followin' your orders." Then as she looked at him blankly he smiled and explained: "He's paintin' new letters to her name—she's goin' to be the *Diana-Kate* from now on. Guess you an' that old heathen lady goddess might's well get used to each other, for you're goin' to have about eleven months of keepin' close company three astern."

And so our voyage began.

IN WHICH WE GO TO SEA

That night Phoebe and I spent on a horsehair sofa of extraordinary slipperiness in the aftercabin of the *Diana-Kate*. Later, Phoebe was to have a berth fitted for her in the Captain's quarters, but our coming had been so unexpected there was time for nothing besides getting the vessel in readiness to weigh anchor.

"I aim to put out by four," I heard Captain Preble telling the man that Andy had called the mate, "and we'll make the tide serve us out."

I remember his words distinctly, for I considered it very obliging of the tide to be willing to serve us. It amazes me to think how ignorant I was then of the simplest sea phrases.

All that night as Phoebe and I slid and slipped on the horsehair, I listened to the strange sounds which were to become familiar to me for many months. Such rattlings and squeakings, and such grinding of chains and clumpings of boots on the wooden decks overhead. There were cries, as well, that I could not make out. It was all very enlivening.

When Phoebe carried me up the steep steps of the companion-way and on deck next morning, we found the *Diana-Kate* running before the wind. Her square sails were billowing out in fine fashion and her bow dipped and rose to be lifted by great blue-green combers the like of which I had never seen before.

"Huh, this ain't nothin'," Andy told us, as Phoebe nearly lost her footing when the deck suddenly seemed to slip from under her, "you just wait till we get 'round by ol' Hatt'ras an' then you'll see somethin'."

"A lot you know 'bout Hatt'ras, young man," said a deep voice nearby, and a big man in faded blue trousers and shirt stopped beside us, "you run along down to the galley and help same's you're here for. Scud now."

Andy scudded as he was told. He disappeared down the stairs we had just climbed and presently the smell of coffee began to mingle with the sea air. The big sailor lifted Phoebe to a seat on a carpenter's wooden bench. This stood amidships near what I later learned were the try-works but which then looked to me only like deep pits of brick built into the deck between the masts. Several men were working nearby at odd jobs. They were all brown and big like the first.

"Well, so we've got ladies aboard this trip, eh, Bill?" one greeted us, giving Phoebe a knowing wink as he made the most intricate knottings of rope between his fingers. "S'pose that means we'll have to mind our P's and Q's?"

Phoebe was being measured for the new bunk she was to sleep in and I for a little rope hammock which the sailor named Elija, called 'Lige for short, had promised to make me. They were so jolly and friendly and the strong sea sunshine felt so good, with the wind blowing and the big ballooning sails throwing shadows on each other, that I felt only pleasure as I looked out upon the miles of tossing blue waters before us–not a single regret to see the far hump of land that was Boston disappearing from sight.

Phoebe was only a little seasick those first days out, the rest of us not at all. Andy sang and whistled and danced hornpipes the crew taught him. Even Mrs. Preble grew more resigned to the cramped quarters of the ship's galley and made a batch of molasses cookies big enough for all, a rare treat indeed for a whaling ship, or for any vessel, in those days.

Although there were still one or two who grumbled and made dire predictions about the presence of women aboard a whaler, we were for the most part treated with real consideration. In fact, Phoebe Preble and I were soon on such friendly terms with various members of the crew that her mother complained there would be no living with the child when we got home again. I, too, felt a distinct sense of my own importance when 'Lige and his special crony, one Reuben Somes, said that they had no doubt I would bring them good luck on this voyage. They decided this after Phoebe had told them the story of my being made of mountain-ash wood.

"Why, now, she'd ought to be as much good to us as old lady Diana down yonder," Reuben said, pointing toward the carved figurehead just under the bowsprit.

I must confess that I felt a little frightened lest he should suggest that I too be nailed in a like position, to be drenched in salt spray whenever the vessel took any particularly big wave. I did not envy the poor lady. I was far too graceful for all my privileges, especially for the little hammock 'Lige had made me. I had other presents as well, for the men all seemed to be clever at making things from odds and ends of rope, chips, or bits of wood. They vied with one another at fitting me out, and before we were many weeks out I possessed not only a hammock to sleep in but also a chip basket, a carved bone footstool, and a sea chest to hold all my possessions. This last was the gift of Bill Buckle, who spared no pains to make it perfect in every respect. It was painted a beautiful bright blue, with proper rope handles at each end and my initials, H. P., picked out in shiny nail heads on the lid. That was a proud day for me, and Phoebe was so pleased she ran all over the ship exhibiting it. She was all for climbing up to the crow's nest to show the lookout, but her father soon put a stop to that.

The Cat Who Went to Heaven

Elizabeth Coatsworth

—•• NEWBERY MEDAL, 1931 ••—

A LITTLE CAT BECOMES A CONSTANT COMPANION TO A POOR AND COMPASSIONATE JAPANESE ARTIST.

Once upon a time, far away in Japan, a poor young artist sat alone in his little house, waiting for his dinner. His housekeeper had gone to market, and he sat sighing to think of all the things he wished she would bring home. He expected her to hurry in at any minute, bowing and opening her little basket to show him how wisely she had spent their few pennies. He heard her step and jumped up. He was very hungry!

But the housekeeper lingered by the door, and the basket stayed shut.

"Come," he cried, "what's in the basket?"

The housekeeper trembled and held the basket tight in two hands. "It has seemed to me, sir," she said, "that we are very lonely here."

"Lonely!" said the artist. "I should think so! How can we have guests when we have nothing to offer them? It is so long since I have tasted rice cakes that I forgot what they taste like!" And he sighed again, for he loved rice cakes, and dumplings, and little cakes filled with sweet bean jelly. He loved tea served in fine china cups, in company with some friend, seated on flat cushions, talking perhaps about a spray of peach blossoms standing like a little princess in an alcove. But weeks and weeks had gone by since anyone had bought even the smallest picture. The poor artist was glad enough to have rice and a coarse fish now and then. If he did not sell another picture soon, he would not have even that. His eyes went back to the basket. Perhaps the old woman had managed to pick up a turnip or two, or even a peach, too ripe to haggle long over.

"Sir," said the housekeeper, seeing the direction of his look, "it has often seemed to me that I was kept awake by rats."

At that the artist laughed out loud.

"Rats?" he repeated. "Rats? My dear old woman, no rats come to such a poor house as this where not the smallest crumb falls to the mats."

Then he looked at the housekeeper and a dreadful suspicion filled his mind.

"You have brought us home nothing to eat!" he said.

"True, master," said the old woman sorrowfully.

"You have brought us home a cat!" said the artist.

"My master knows everything!" answered the housekeeper bowing low.

Then the artist jumped to his feet, and strode up and down the room, and pulled his hair, and it seemed to him that he would die of hunger and anger.

"A cat? A cat?" he cried. "Have you gone mad? Here we are starving and you must bring home a goblin, a goblin to share the little we have and perhaps to suck our blood at night! Yes! It will be fine to wake up in the dark and feel teeth at our throats and look into eyes as big as lanterns! But perhaps you are right! Perhaps we are so miserable it would be a good thing to have us die at once, and be carried over the ridgepoles in the jaws of a devil!"

"But, master, master, there are many good cats, too!" cried the poor old woman. "Have you forgotten the little boy who drew all the pictures of cats on the screens of the deserted temple and then went to sleep in a closet and heard such a racket in the middle of the night? And in the morning when he awoke again, he found the giant rat lying dead, master—the rat who had come to kill him! Who destroyed the rat, sir, tell me that? It was his own cats, there they sat on the screen as he had drawn them, but there was blood on their claws! And he became a great artist like yourself. Surely, there are many good cats, master."

Then the old woman began to cry. The artist stopped and looked at her as the tears fell from her bright black eyes and ran down the wrinkles in her cheeks. Why should he be angry? He had gone hungry before.

"Well, well," he said, "sometimes it is good fortune to have even a devil in the household. It keeps other devils away. Now I suppose this cat of yours will wish to eat. Perhaps it may arrange for us to have some food in the house. Who knows? We can't be worse off than we are."

The housekeeper bowed very low in gratitude.

"There is not a kinder heart in the whole town than my master's," she said, and prepared to carry the covered basket into the kitchen.

But the artist stopped her. Like all artists he was curious.

"Let us see the creature," he said, pretending he scarcely cared whether he saw it or not.

So the old woman put down the basket and opened the lid. Nothing happened for a moment. Then a round, pretty white head came slowly above the bamboo, and two big yellow eyes looked around the room, and a little white paw appeared on the rim. Suddenly, without moving the basket at all, a little white cat jumped out on the mats and stood there as a person might stand who scarcely knew if she were welcome. Now that the cat was out of the basket, the artist saw that she had yellow and black spots on her sides, a little tail like a rabbit's, and that she did everything daintily.

"Oh, a three-colored cat," said the artist. "Why didn't you say so from the beginning? They are very lucky, I understand."

As soon as the little cat heard him speak so kindly, she walked over to him and bowed down her head as though she were saluting him, while the old woman clapped her hands for joy. The artist forgot that he was hungry. He had seen nothing so lovely as their cat for a long time.

"She will have to have a name," he declared, sitting down again on the old matting while the cat stood sedately before him. "Let me see: She is like new snow dotted with gold pieces and lacquer; she is like a white flower on which butterflies of two kinds have alighted; she is like–"

But here he stopped. For a sound like a teakettle crooning on the fire was filling his little room.

"How contented!" sighed the artist. "This is better than rice." Then he said to the housekeeper, "We have been lonely, I see now."

"May I humbly suggest," said the housekeeper, "that we call this cat Good Fortune?"

Somehow the name reminded the artist of all his troubles.

"Anything will do," he said, getting up and tightening his belt over his empty stomach, "but take her to the kitchen now, out of the way." No sooner were the words out of his mouth than the little cat rose and walked away, softly and meekly.

THE FIRST SONG OF THE HOUSEKEEPER

I'm poor and I'm old,
My hair has gone gray,
My robe is all patches,
My sash is not gay.

The fat God of Luck
Never enters our door,
And no visitors come
To drink tea anymore.

Yet I hold my head high
As I walk through the town
While I serve such a master
My heart's now bowed down!

The next morning the artist found the cat curled up in a ball on his cushion.

"Ah! the softest place, I see!" said he. Good Fortune immediately rose and, moving away, began to wash herself with the greatest thoroughness and dexterity. When the housekeeper came back from market and cooked the small meal, Good Fortune did not go near the store, though her eyes wandered toward it now and then and her thistledown whiskers quivered slightly with hunger. She happened to be present when the old woman brought in a low table and set it before her master. Next came a bowl of fish soup—goodness knows how the housekeeper must have wheedled to get that fish!—but Good Fortune made a point of keeping her eyes in the other direction.

"One would say," said the artist, pleased by her behavior, "that she understood it is not polite to stare at people while they eat. She has been very properly brought up. From whom did you buy her?"

"I bought her from a fisherman in the market," said the old woman. "She is the eldest daughter of his chief cat. You know a junk never puts out to sea without a cat to frighten away the water devils."

"Pooh!" said the artist. "A cat doesn't frighten devils. They are kin. The sea demons spare a ship out of courtesy to the cat, not from fear of her."

The old woman did not contradict. She knew her place better than that. Good Fortune continued to sit with her face to the wall.

The artist took another sip or two of soup. Then he said to the housekeeper, "Please be king enough to bring a bowl for Good Fortune when you bring my rice. She must be hungry."

When the bowl came he called her politely. Having been properly invited, Good Fortune stopped looking at the other side of the room and came to sit beside her master. She took care not to eat hurriedly and soil her white round chin. Although she must have been very hungry, she would eat only half her rice. It was as though she kept the rest for the next day, wishing to be no more of a burden than she could help.

So the days went. Each morning the artist knelt quietly on a mat and painted beautiful little pictures that no one bought: some of warriors with two swords; some of lovely ladies doing up their long curtains of hair; some of the demons of the wind blowing out their cheeks; and some little laughable ones of rabbits running in the moonlight, or fat badgers beating on their stomachs like drums. While he worked, the old woman went to market with a few of their remaining pennies; she spent the rest of her time in cooking, washing, scrubbing, and darning to keep their threadbare house and their threadbare clothes together. Good Fortune, having found out that she was unable to help either of them, sat quietly in the sun, ate as little as she could, and often spent hours with lowered head before the image of the Buddha on its low shelf.

"She is praying to the Enlightened One," said the housekeeper in admiration.

"She is catching flies," said the artist. "You would believe anything wonderful of your spotted cat." Perhaps he was a little ashamed to remember how seldom he prayed now when his heart felt so heavy.

But one day he was forced to admit that Good Fortune was not like other cats. He was sitting in his especial room watching sparrows fly in and out of the hydrangea bushes outside when he saw Good Fortune leap from a shadow and catch a bird. In a second the brown wings, the black-capped head, the legs like briers, the frightened eyes, were between her paws. The artist would have clapped his hands and tried to scare her away, but before he had time to make the least move, he saw Good Fortune hesitate and then slowly, slowly, lift first one white paw and then another from the sparrow. Unhurt, in a loud whir of wings, the bird flew away.

"What mercy!" cried the artist, and the tears came into his eyes. Well he knew his cat must be hungry and well he knew what hunger felt like. "I am ashamed when I think I called such a cat a goblin," he thought. "Why, she is more virtuous than a priest."

It was just then, at that very moment, that the old housekeeper appeared, trying hard to hide her excitement.

"Master!" she said as soon as she could find words. "Master! The head priest from the temple himself is here in the next room and wishes to see you. What, oh, what do you think His Honor has come here for?"

"The priest from the temple wishes to see me?" repeated the artist, scarcely able to believe his ears, for the priest was a very important person, not one likely to spend his time in visiting poor artists whom nobody thought much of. When the housekeeper had nodded her head until it nearly fell off, the artist felt as excited as she did. But he forced himself to be calm.

"Run! run!" he exclaimed. "Buy tea and cakes" and he pressed into the old woman's hands the last thing of value he owned, the vase that stood in the alcove of his room and always held a branch or spray of flowers. But even if his room must be bare after this, the artist did not hesitate: No guest could be turned away without proper entertainment. He was ashamed to think that he had kept the priest waiting for even a minute and had not seen him coming and welcomed him at the door. He scarcely felt Good Fortune rub encouragingly against his ankles as he hurried off.

In the next room the priest sat, lost in meditation. The artist bowed low before him, drawing in his breath politely, and then waited to be noticed. It seemed to him a century before the priest lifted his head and the far-off look went out of his eyes. Then the artist bowed again and said that his house was honored forever by so holy a presence.

The priest wasted no time in coming to the point.

"We desire," said he, "a painting of the death of our Lord Buddha for the temple. There was some discussion as to the artist, so we put slips of paper, each marked with a name, before the central image in the great hall, and in the morning all the slips had blown away except yours. So we knew Buddha's will in the matter. Hearing something of your circumstances, I have brought a first payment with me so that you may relieve your mind of worry while at your work. Only a clear pool has beautiful reflections. If the work is successful, as we hope, your fortune is made, for what the temple approves becomes the fashion in the town." With that the priest drew a heavy purse from his belt.

The artist never remembered how he thanked the priest, or served him the ceremonial tea, or bowed him to his narrow gate. Here at last was a chance for fame and fortune. He felt that this might be all a dream. Why had the Buddha chosen him? He had been too sad to pray often and the housekeeper too busy—could it be that Buddha would listen to the prayers of a little spotted cat? He was afraid that he would wake up and find that the whole thing was an apparition and that the purse was filled with withered leaves. Perhaps he never would have come to himself if he had not been roused by a very curious noise.

It was a double kind of noise. It was not exactly like any noise that the artist had ever heard. The artist, who was always curious, went into the kitchen to see what could be making the sound, and there, sure enough, were the housekeeper and Good Fortune, and one was crying for joy and one was purring for joy, and it would have been hard to have said which was making more noise. At that the artist had to laugh out loud, but it was not his old sad sort of laugh. This was like a boy's—and he took them both into his arms. Then there were three sounds of joy in the poor old kitchen.

Calico Bush

Rachel Field

—∗• Newbery Honor, 1932 •∗—

Set in 1743, this is a classic pioneer story about thirteen-year-old Marguerite Ledoux, a French orphan who is "bound" for six years to the Sargent family, which is about to start a farm on the isolated coast of Maine.

1743 and a fine June morning. Blue water, wind from the southwest, and Marguerite Ledoux taking her last sight of Marblehead as she crouched at the low railing of the *Isabella B.* Farther astern she could see Amos Hunt, master and owner of the *Isabella B.*, at the tiller, with Joel Sargent and his brother, Ira, handling ropes or helping to stow their goods more compactly. Nearer at hand Joel's wife, Dolly Sargent, was seated on an old wooden chest, her eyes also straining against the strong sea sunshine till the last familiar headland should be out of sight. Four small children clustered about her, and a baby filled her broad lap. In her full, brown homespun dress and scoop bonnet, Marguerite thought she looked mightily like one of the hens in their coop up forward. But of this resemblance she said nothing, having learned that Bound-out Girls were not expected to hold opinions of their own, least of all upon the appearance of their masters and mistresses.

"Maggie! Maggie!" She started up, seeing Dolly beckoning to her, remembering of a sudden that this was to be her name now.

"Here's a great hank o' wool to be untangled and wound," Dolly Sargent was saying. "No need to idle the morning away if we *are* bound for dear knows where."

Dolly sighed, and her eyes turned once more to the low line of shore that grew steadily a dimmer, paler blue as the boat carried them on.

Taking the wool from her, the girl moved back to her place amidships. Here she found a small wooden keg between several larger ones and sat down to her task. Her fingers were brown and twiglike, but they moved deftly in and out of the thick blue strands of wool. The sun was higher now, and she pushed the cotton bonnet back on her shoulders, making the strings of it fast against the breeze.

Presently a sandy-headed boy went by with a great leap, tweaking one of her dark braids as he passed, and wrinkling his face up into a wide grimace.

"Ho, Frenchee!" he sang out shrilly, "you'll be black's an Injun 'fore we make port."

The girl did not reply, bending to her work more steadily, though she felt an odd dread as always at the approach of this boy. Caleb Sargent was thirteen, only a few months older than she would be on her next birthday, but he stood a good head and a half above her, and his keen blue eyes and teasing mouth were forever expressing his scorn of all womankind and of Marguerite Ledoux in particular. Sometimes she imagined that he also felt an outsider in the midst of this clamoring group of younger half-sisters and his half-brother. His own mother, Joel Sargent's first wife, had died years before. This morning he was feeling very proud of himself, partly because he had inherited a pair of his Uncle Ira's nankeen breeches, still several sizes too large for him, and partly because he had been given charge of the family livestock—the cow and her calf, the hens and chickens, and four unhappy sheep who kept up a pitiful bleating in the forward part of the ship. With some old planks he had been knocking up a makeshift pen for them. Now he scrambled back to this rough shelter with a twist of rope he had begged of his father.

Captain Hunt watched him go with a dubious headshake.

"Ain't likely to make the headway we'd ought to with such a load forward," he was complaining for the twentieth time since they had put out. "I didn't lot on carrying livestock and all these here young ones when we made our bargain."

"Never you mind that," Joel answered him shortly, "I paid you what you asked in hard silver, every shilling of it, and if you ain't aiming to do your part—"

"Dad blast ye!" the Captain broke in. "I'm not the man to go back on my word once it's given. But I say she sets too low in the water. She ain't trimmed proper."

Words passed between the men. There was more argument as to the shifting of household goods stowed in the cockpit and under cover of the hatches.

It was strange, Marguerite thought, to see the family spinning wheel and churn lashed to the rail along with a chest and settle, and the feather bed and a couple of patchwork quilts spread on wooden benches below in the dark little cabin. Where the light struck through the hatchway, she could make out the bright reds and greens of "The Rose of Sharon" and "The Feathered Star," both familiar patterns and greatly cherished by Dolly Sargent, who had little time nowadays for such fine needlework. Overhead the great canvas sail filled and strained as the *Isabella B.* scudded before the wind. There were patches upon it too—sharp, white lengths of new canvas set into the older weathered gray. One of these showed jagged and triangular as if a dart of lightning had left its mark there.

A sturdily built boat, the *Isabella B.*, larger and heavier than most of the fishing smacks thereabouts, with a blunt-nosed prow that rose dripping with salt spray only to plunge and rise again. An odd-shaped world of wood and rope and canvas in which eleven souls and all their earthly possessions were to live for upwards of five days and nights. Strange indeed, but perhaps no stranger than what had already befallen Marguerite Ledoux in the last twelve months.

She was thinking of this as her fingers moved through the wool, trying to sort out the events that had brought her by varying stages to being there at the beck and call of a family of strangers, on a wooden vessel bound for parts unknown—as unknown to her, at least, she told herself, as these new colonies across the sea had been when she and Grand'mère and Oncle Pierre had set forth all those many months before. It had been just such another blue day, and the port of Le Havre had been brave to see in the morning light. Grand'mère had cried, seeing the last of France, but Oncle Pierre had been in good spirits. He had laughed and planned many things—the house they should have together someday in a part called after King Louis, where it was warm and sunny, with rich lands, where people talked their language and one would fancy oneself in a Little France. There they would pay well to hear him play his violin, and it would certainly not be long before he taught those rich planters' sons and daughters the latest dancing steps. Yes, Oncle Pierre would be a personage there, perhaps the only French dancing master in the New World. The thought had made him hold his head very high and point his toes out even when their ship pitched and the deck grew wet and slanting.

Even Grand'mère had grown resigned and happy, thinking of Oncle Pierre a great man over in Little France, thinking of the new home they would make for Marguerite, whose own dead parents had left her in their hands. It had been a long, long voyage, with sun and storm and fog and variable winds, but they had not minded.

Even with food grown scanty and water-soaked they had not minded very much. There were always the plans to talk about among themselves, or if the nights were fine and the sky alive with stars large and small, there had been Oncle Pierre's violin to make music. Such beautiful music as he would play, and so many old songs he knew, both the words and tunes. Sitting there now in the shadow of the *Isabella B.*'s patched sail, Marguerite could sing those same little notes and repeat the same words he had taught her; and yet, for all that, Oncle Pierre was dead and gone. He would never point his toes in their narrow shoes again, nor draw his bow smoothly across the taut strings.

It had happened with the swiftness of lightning. One of the sailors had fallen ill almost within sight of land. Great red sores had appeared on his face, and fever burned in his eyes. It had been a terrible time. One had scarcely dared to look at another's face for fear of seeing the first dread sign. And then Oncle Pierre—Marguerite could not even now let herself think of the day when he had fallen ill. They would not allow her and Grand'mère to go near him. Two old sailors with scarred faces did what they could. But it had been no use at all. She and Grand'mère knelt together on the deck when they buried him at sea; they told over their rosaries and whispered what prayers they could. After that, the Captain put them ashore at the nearest port. It was not the one intended, but the Captain would take no more risks. He must be rid of his ailing crew and clean his vessel. All Oncle Pierre's belongings had been flung into the sea with him, even the precious violin and bow, so she and Grand'mère had nothing but their clothes and the little money bag with its few remaining coins.

There had been none to welcome them to the port of Marblehead, and Grand'mère was too spent to journey to that far place, named for King Louis, where she would have heard her own tongue. So it was one lodging after another while their money lasted, and then a place called "Poor Farm," which they shared with others even less fortunate. But Grand'mère had ceased to care much by that time. She was too weak to get up from her bed, and often she imagined for days on end that she was in France again. At such times she smiled and sang snatches of the songs Oncle Pierre had sung, and if she forgot the words, Marguerite would join in as she sat beside her with sewing. For Marguerite could sew very well for a girl of twelve. All the women at the Poor Farm had praised her little stitches, and she had showed them how to do fancy scallops and garlands as the Sisters in the convent at Le Havre had taught her. In return they helped her care for Grand'mère, and gave her instruction in their language. It had not been hard to learn, although people still smiled to hear the way she said certain words. There was Caleb, for instance, who never tired of mocking her queer r's and the way she could never say her h's.

Remembering Caleb, she looked quickly forward, relieved to see his shock of orange-colored hair bent over the coops. All the rest being busy also, she took this moment to draw from under the front of her dress of coarse gray holland a piece of cord from which hung two small objects. One of these was a plain gold ring, the same that Grand'mère had always worn, the other a button of gilt from Oncle Pierre's best blue coat. She had found it afterwards between two boards of the deck where it had rolled. Such little things, she thought, to have outlasted Grand'mère and Oncle Pierre. Now they were all that remained to her of her past, and as such they were very precious.

People had been kind to her when Grand'mère died, but afterwards they had explained that life would be very different. It was not enough, it appeared, for one to know songs and dancing steps and how to sew and embroider. This was a new, rough country with very different sort of work to be done, and an able-bodied girl of twelve must earn her "board and keep." She remembered what a frightening sound those same words had had. And then they had explained to her that she was to be a "Bound-out Girl." Already those in authority were searching about for a family who would take her to work for them. But the fact that she was French had stood in her way. Several women had come to look her over, only to dismiss her with headshakes when they discovered her birth.

"We want no flighty foreign critters under our roof," she had heard one woman say.

The other had expressed like disapproval and had even hinted that with King George at war with the French across the water, she wouldn't feel she was doing her duty to consort with the enemy. But Joel Sargent and Dolly had not been so particular.

"Another pair of hands and feet are what we're in need of," they had explained, "and so long's she ain't the contrary kind we'll over-look where she was born and raised."

Marguerite had sat by while the papers were being drawn up and signed. She had not understood many of the strange words and phrases, but she had not missed their meaning. From that day till her eighteenth birthday she was theirs to command. She would be answerable to these people for her every act and word, bound to serve them for six long years in return for shelter, food, and such garments as should be deemed necessary.

Hastily she slipped the cord and its treasures out of sight again and, tucking her bare feet under her, went at the wool more vigor-ously.

This had been in March. Now it was June. Marblehead was well behind them. Save to herself she was no longer Marguerite Ledoux but the Sargents' Bound-out Girl in gray holland and cotton sun-bonnet, who answered to the name of Maggie when called.

Her mistress was calling to her now, "Here, Maggie, mind the young ones while I fetch the men some victuals. Their stomachs must be clean empty, their tongues are that quarrelsome."

Marguerite rose quickly to take the baby, and the children flocked about her in turn, their sturdy fairness in marked contrast to her own dark coloring and wiry build. Becky and Susan, the six-year-old twins, were alike as two peas in a pod, a stocky pair with stiff little braids of yellow hair and blue eyes. They too wore sun-bonnets and dresses of gray holland, short in the sleeve and neck but gathered round the waist into full skirts that flapped about their bare ankles. Patty came next in order, being four, with Jacob, three, ever close at her heels. Their hair, white and curly as lambs' wool, was sheared close to their round heads, and save for Jacob's short breeches and dimpled chin they too might have passed for twins. The baby, Deborah, called Debby by them all, was eight months old and already showed tufts of light hair under her tight little cap. Her eyes were also very blue and her cheeks apple-round and rosy.

"Keep her out the sun, much as you can," the baby's mother cautioned from the cabin. "It's hot enough to raise blisters on her, and this is no place for her to run a fever, dear knows."

"Yes'm," Marguerite answered as she had been taught, crooking her arm to shade the baby's face.

"This old floor's so hot it burns my feet, it does," complained Becky, standing first on one foot and then on the other.

"You should spread your dress out," Marguerite told her, "and then if you fold your feet under you when you sit, you will not feel it."

She showed them how to do so, and they crouched beside her, all but Jacob, who climbed to the larger keg and sat with his feet stuck straight before him staring out to sea.

"Prenez garde!" Marguerite cried, as the boat swung about and the child all but slid off. Then, seeing the blank looks on the small faces before her, she caught herself up quickly: "Take care to hold fast!"

"Yes," echoed Susan, "and take care the boom do not sweep you over the side when they shift it."

They were used to boats, as were most seaport children of that day, and although Jacob was only three he was expected to look out for himself. He did not, however, remain long on his perch, for Caleb, happening by, picked him off by the back of his shirt and set him down with his sisters.

"I'll send you to join the fishes if you don't watch out," he chided before he hurried over to the men about the tiller.

They were discussing charts and courses as they ate thick pieces of bread and cheese out of Dolly Sargent's basket, washing it down with draughts of beer from a keg the Captain had brought aboard.

"There ain't no two ways about it." The Captain spoke up at last. "We'll stick to the inner course if it takes us a week from here to the Penobscot. When I said we'd go outside the shoals I didn't lot on havin' her so down by the head."

"Then we'd best put in at Falmouth," Joel said, pointing with his big leathery forefinger to a place on the chart spread between them. "We'll be 'most out of water and feed for the critters by then."

"Yes," agreed Ira, "it'll give us all a chance to stretch our legs a bit, and Dolly won't look so glum if she knows she'll have another sight of folks and fashions." He smiled his long, slow smile, cutting off a hunk of tobacco from a plug he carried.

"I guess it'll be my last sight of them, and no mistake," she answered him with a sigh. "'Twas hard enough takin' leave of Marble-head, but I declare I'd feel 'most content to settle down in any huddle of houses now."

"That's the woman of it," her husband retorted. "Neighbors and gossiping from morning till night—that's all you can think about. But when it gets so settled a body can see houses on three sides from his own door then I say it's time to be off where there's land to spare."

"Plenty of elbow room, that's what a man needs," put in Ira. "I was commencin' to feel cooped up in Marblehead long afore that man happened along to sell you his eastern land."

"Lots of folks never know when they're well off," Dolly remarked sagely between bites of bread.

"And lots would live and die on a measly acre or two when they might help themselves to a couple o' hundred." There was a light in Joel's eyes that showed he had already taken possession of those new lands. His great hands were crooked a little as if they itched to hold an ax. "Marblehead was gettin' so full of folks you couldn't rightly stir about in it. Sometime the harbor was so cluttered 'twas as much as you could do to edge a dory in; and the highway the same, with such a lot o' coaches and rigs 'twas a caution to cross it."

"Well, you won't be troubled in no such ways where you're a-goin'." Old Captain Hunt wagged his head knowingly. "If folks depended on coaches to go places there, they wouldn't get very far—no, by Godfrey, they wouldn't!"

"I'm not so sot on farmin' as Joel here," Ira went on, "but I figure if you're by the sea you can always make out."

"You're right about that," the Captain agreed. "You'll never want if you're near salt water. It does you for food and takes you places without waitin' for no road."

His last words jogged Marguerite into sudden interest. She had been listening to the talk idly, her eyes on the endlessly parting waves that the *Isabella B.* plowed through. Now she knew in a twinkling what the Captain had meant. The sea was a road, too—a great, watery highway going all round the world. You had only to put out upon it, and it would take you wherever you wanted to go. She smiled to herself, thinking of it so, likening the hollows between the waves to ruts, and themselves moving over it in a coach without wheels.

Now Dolly Sargent was dividing the remains of the bread between the children, breaking it into as many parts as there were mouths, and smearing each piece with molasses from the sweet-smelling wooden piggin. Caleb was sent to milk the cow for Debby, who had awakened crying.

Soon he was back with a hollowed gourd full, warm from old Brindle. The neck of the gourd had been scooped and perforated to make a nursing bottle, and Dolly Sargent let the milk fall drop by drop into the baby's puckered mouth.

"Take the young ones out from under foot, Maggie," Joel told her. "I can't have 'em raisin' a racket hereabouts."

"And watch out Patty and Joel don't gaum theirselves all over with molasses," cautioned their mother, "for the Lord knows when I'll get to wash them clean again."

They found a spot in the shadow of the settle and other house-

hold goods. Here Marguerite returned to her wool-winding, keeping an eye on the four beside her. Becky and Susan got out their
most cherished possession, a corncob doll dressed in a scrap of
bright calico, while Patty busied herself with a handful of shells and
Jacob pulled up imaginary fish with a bit of rope dangling over the
side.

Toward evening the wind changed. It was necessary to tack and
veer continually to make any sort of headway. Captain Hunt kept
up his grumbling about their overloading and squinted warily at a
low bank of clouds the setting sun turned to a fiery rose.

"Those there clouds are lee-set," he muttered. "They'll mean no
good to us."

But for all that the evening was fine and clear. Twilight held long
over the water, and with the sun down the air grew cool. After they
had all eaten what remained in Dolly's basket and the children had
had a drink of milk all round, the three youngest went below to the
tiny cabin. Their mother returned from putting them to bed on the
hard benches. For a while she sat with Marguerite and the twins,
watching darkness come over the water and the first stars appear,
very large and sharply pointed. Presently Ira joined them, and even
Caleb did not feel it beneath his dignity to draw near.

"There's the new moon," said Becky, pointing to a pale sickle
that hung low in the west. "I made a wish on it."

"So did I make a wish on it, myself," Susan said, not wanting to
be outdone. "An' they do say if you bow to it nine times you'll get
what you wished for." She began bobbing her head so fast her
braids jerked up and down stiffly.

"If I had *my* wish," sighed Dolly Sargent, "this here boat would
be headin' back the way we come from."

Marguerite heard Caleb sniff at these words, but before he could
make any retort, Ira Sargent spoke up in his slow, pleasant voice.

"Ever hear tell 'bout the moon an' the powder horn?" he asked.
"An old man told me once, an' he got it from his Granpa back in
Scotland."

"Tell us, Uncle Ira, go on." The two little girls pressed closer to him, their eyes bright in the half darkness.

"It was this-a-way," he told them. "Once there was a man out huntin' an' he went a long, long ways, so far he got tired with night comin' on an' all. So he stretched himself out to sleep. But first he reached up an' hung his powder horn up on a little bright yellow hook that he seen hangin' right over his head. Well, he shut up his eyes an' he went to sleep, but come mornin' when he woke his powder horn was gone. Look high he did, an' look low, an' there weren't nary a sign of it."

"What did he do then?" asked the twins together.

"Weren't nothin' he could do, 'cept go home without it," their uncle went on. "But next evenin' when it got dark he went back to that place where he slept, an' there right over his head was the new moon with his powder horn a-hangin' on it, hooked as nice as could be! So he reached up an' took it back home again."

"Mercy, Ira," chided Dolly Sargent. "You hadn't ought to fill their heads with such foolishness."

Marguerite smiled to herself under cover of the darkness. She felt glad of Ira Sargent and his stories. They made her think of those Grand'mère had told her so often of an evening. She was sorry when he left with Caleb to help light the lanterns from a fire kept burning in an iron kettle. Dolly Sargent went below, but the twins and she sat on together, their bodies huddled close against the sea chill, their eyes on the star-spattered sky overhead. Many planets and constellations she knew from the nights when Oncle Pierre had taught her to call them by name. These she pointed out to the children, naming them over familiarly as one would mention neighbors.

"See, there is Mademoiselle Vénus. Is she not beautiful tonight? And Monsieur Orion with his belt of little stars, and Les Pléiades over yonder."

Presently their mother called the twins to come below, and Marguerite reluctantly followed. She would far rather have stayed out there as the men were preparing to do than creep between the sleeping children in such narrow, box-like quarters. Even when she had settled herself on one of the hard benches with her head on a bag of meal, she lay awake long after all the young Sargents and their mother were asleep. Through the open hatch she could see a bit of the night sky. A fitful brightness came from the stern lantern as it swung with the vessel's motions, and now and again the moving shadows of the men showed as they handled ropes and shifted sail. She could tell from the sound of their voices whether they were talking among themselves or whether the Captain had issued orders. Sometimes she heard Caleb also, his boyish tones shrill against the deeper ones of the three men.

She slept at last, only to waken to shouted orders and a great pitching and rolling. The *Isabella B.* was behaving in a very different manner from her earlier one. Her beams shivered and shook, her bows plunged and reared, and her mast seemed about to be snapped off short at any moment.

"Ciel!" she cried, starting up in the darkness, one hand instinctively reaching for her rosary beads. Remembering in an instant that she no longer possessed any, she slipped from between the children, who lay in a warm heap of arms and legs about her, and made for the hatchway.

How she got up the steps she did not know. Icy-cold water poured down them, and the whole place was awash. The *Isabella B.* was careening at such an angle that it was impossible to keep a footing except by clinging to the rails and inching along. She could make out the figure of Joel Sargent crawling in this fashion to join Ira, who was struggling to reef in the canvas. Captain Hunt clung valiantly to the tiller, though waves swirled up and about him till it seemed he must be swept away with each fresh deluge. As he threw his weight against the tiller, he shouted out orders to the others. But the noise of wind and water was such that even his deep-sea voice sounded faint and broken.

"Make the stays fast!" Marguerite heard him bellowing, and

then the next moment when he caught sight of her, it was, "Below! Keep below there!"

She would have obeyed had it not been for a sudden shrill cry from the bow. Caleb and the livestock were in trouble. She knew this without the splintering of wood and the terrified lows and bleats to warn her. Hardly realizing what she was doing, Marguerite set herself to go forward. Flattening her body against the side of the cabin she edged along, clinging with one hand to the low wooden rail, and bracing her bare feet against any board that could help her keep a foothold. Whatever headway she gained she must make in the second of lull between the waves. They swept over and about her, filling her nose and mouth with salt water. The wind whipped at her wet braids, but she hung on. The men shouted to her; she was past heeding.

Halfway along, a particularly high wave washed over the straining bows, burying them in spray. Seeing it upon them, Marguerite lowered her head, flinging all her strength into the grip of her hands and feet. There came another sharp cry from Caleb, and she looked up in time to see a white mass swept overboard. She did not need the agonized bleating to tell her what it was.

Caleb's makeshift pen had been washed away, but the forward rail still held. Somehow he had managed to lash the cow and her calf to this. By twisting his own body between these ropes he kept himself from going over the side, while with both arms he struggled to hold the three remaining sheep. Earlier in the day their legs had been hobbled, the fore and hind ones being tied together to keep the animals quiet. Now this only increased their helplessness. They were like so many bags of wool at the mercy of every wave. Even as Marguerite crept nearer, there came another lurch and Caleb lost his hold on one. Without knowing how she did it, she freed one hand and clutched at the woolly body.

"Keep a-holt!" she heard Caleb shouting in her ear, and she dug her fingers tighter into the thick wool.

They could barely make each other out in the dark and wet, but the whiteness of the sheep helped to mark the places where they clung. Now and again in any slight lull they shouted a word or so to show that they still hung on. But for the most part neither had any breath to spare.

"Ah, my arm—you will twist it off!" gasped Marguerite as the sheep struggled in a panic of animal terror.

She caught her lips between her teeth lest Caleb should hear her crying with the pain. After a little it did not hurt so much. Either the sheep had tired itself, or she had grown used to the strain. She felt very cold and numb and almost too spent to be afraid when the *Isabella B.* took some especially high sea or plunged from watery height to hollow.

And then it was over. The squall passed almost as suddenly as it had come upon them. The wind no longer tore and tugged at the rigging, and in the early light of morning the sea grew quieter. Ira Sargent was the first to reach them. His face looked pale under his sunburn as he peered over the wreckage to see if they were still there. Without a word he took the sheep from Marguerite's hold, leaving her free to crawl aft. She could scarcely grip the wooden rail with her fingers so cramped, and she was too soaked to care that a foot of water slopped about the cabin floor with every lurch and roll.

"Never lotted on seein' that pair of young ones alive," she heard Captain Hunt saying to Joel as she stumbled down the hatchway.

"Well, I guessed Caleb would stick fast," the other answered, "but why *she* ain't gone to bottom traipsin' out there in all that blow is past me. She's got grit, wherever she was raised—I'll say that for her."

"Yes, she's quite a craft, that girl," the Captain added, and then he was shouting orders to Ira about letting out more sail. Marguerite tumbled in a heap on the hard bench below. The children whimpered on all sides, and Dolly Sargent scolded her for her rashness, but this was nothing to the inner glow she felt as she remembered the words she had just heard. The Captain had praised her, and Joel Sargent had admitted that she had grit. Perhaps even Caleb would be less scornful of her now. She fell asleep and dreamed herself back in Le Havre in the sunny garden of the convent. The Sisters were moving about in their soft blue robes and starched headdresses that were like crisped blue wings, and the chapel bell was ringing for noonday mass.

She awoke with a dull ache in her head and a body so stiff it was all she could do to keep from crying out as she painfully climbed from the dark cabin into the brightness above. The sun stood high overhead, and the sea was so smooth and blue it seemed impossible it could ever have buffeted the *Isabella B.* so fiercely. But all about were signs of that struggle. Part of the forward railing was gone. One of the hencoops and more than half the precious household goods had been washed away. Dolly Sargent sat in the midst of the younger children, mourning the loss of her possessions in no uncertain terms, while her husband reminded her that it was a mercy they hadn't all followed them to the bottom.

"You'd best be thankful we saved three o' the sheep," Caleb told her with pride. "But for Maggie an' me there wouldn't be so much as a snag o' wool left."

"An' what good are sheep to me without a spinning wheel?" she answered him shortly, turning one of the quilts the better to dry it in the sun.

"But for all her fault-finding, Dolly Sargent was easy with her Bound-out Girl that day. She set her no tasks beyond looking out for the children and even gave her a bit of tallow to rub on a great bruise that had risen on her forehead. Already it was turning a deep purple, a sight which seemed to gratify Caleb.

"My," he said, "but you're easy battered. Guess I'm tough's a bear, or I'd be black an' blue all over."

"Oh, hush up," his uncle Ira told him good-naturedly. "Whatever it was struck her warn't no feather."

Caddie Woodlawn

Carol Ryrie Brink

—❖ Newbery Medal, 1936 ❖—

Scarcely out of one scrape before she is into another, irrepressible, spirited eleven-year-old Caddie Woodlawn refuses to be a "lady," preferring instead to be a tomboy.

Three Adventurers

In 1864 Caddie Woodlawn was eleven, and as wild a little tomboy as ever ran the woods of western Wisconsin. She was the despair of her mother and of her elder sister, Clara. But her father watched her with a little shine of pride in his eyes, and her brothers accepted her as one of themselves without a question. Indeed, Tom, who was two years older, and Warren, who was two years younger than Caddie, needed Caddie to link them together into an inseparable trio. Together they got in and out of more scrapes and adventures than any one of them could have imagined alone. And in those pioneer days, Wisconsin offered plenty of opportunities for adventure to three wide-eyed, red-headed youngsters.

On a bright Saturday afternoon in the early fall, Tom and Caddie and Warren Woodlawn sat on a bank of the Menomonie River, or Red Cedar as they call it now, taking off their clothes. Their red heads shone in the sunlight. Tom's hair was the darkest, Caddie's the nearest golden, and nine-year-old Warren's was plain carrot color. Not one of the three knew how to swim, but they were going across the river nevertheless. A thin thread of smoke beyond the bend on the other side of the river told them that the Indians were at work on a birch-bark canoe.

"Do you think the Indians around here would ever get mad and massacre folks like they did up north?" wondered Warren, tying his shirt up in a little bundle.

"No, sir," said Tom, "not these Indians!"

"Not Indian John, anyhow," said Caddie. She had just unfastened the many troublesome little buttons on the back of her tight-waisted dress, and, before taking it off, she paused a moment to see if she could balance a fresh-water clam shell on her big toe. She found that she could.

"No, not Indian John!" she repeated decidedly, having got the matter of the clam shell off her mind. "Even if he does have a scalp belt," she added. The thought of the scalp belt always made her hair prickle delightfully up where her scalp lock grew.

"Naw," said Tom, "the fellows who spread those massacre stories are just big-mouthed scared-cats who don't know the Indians, I guess."

"Big-mouthed scared-cats," repeated Warren, admiring Tom's command of language.

"Big-mouthed scared cats," echoed a piping voice from the bank above. Seven-year-old Hetty, who fluttered wistfully on the outer edge of their adventures, filed away Tom's remark in her active brain. It would be useful to tell Mother, some time when Mother was complaining about Tom's language. The three below her paid no attention to Hetty's intrusion. Their red heads, shining in the sunlight, did not even turn in her direction. Hetty's hair was red, too, like Father's, but somehow, in spite of her hair, she belonged on the dark-haired side of the family where Mother and Clara and all the safe and tidy virtues were. She poised irresolutely on the bank above the three adventurous ones. If they had only turned around and looked at her! But they were enough in themselves. She could not make up her mind what to do. She wanted to go with them, and yet she wanted just as much to run home and tell Mother and Clara what they were about to do. Hetty was the self-appointed newsbearer of the family. Wild horses could not prevent her from being the first to tell, whatever it was that happened.

Tom and Caddie and Warren finished undressing, tied their clothes into tight bundles, and stepped out into the river. The water was low after a long, hot summer, but still it looked cold and deep. Hetty shuddered. She had started to undo one shoe, but now she quickly tied it up again. She had made up her mind. She turned around and flew across the fields to tell Mother.

Tom knew from experience that he could just keep his chin above water and touch bottom with his toes across the deep part of the river. It would have been over Caddie's and Warren's heads, but, if they held onto Tom and kept their feet paddling, they could just keep their heads above water. They had done it before. Tom went first with his bundle of clothes balanced on his head. Caddie came next, clutching Tom's shoulder with one hand and holding her bundle of clothes on top of her head with the other. Warren clung to Caddie's shoulder in the same manner, balancing his own clothes with his free hand. They moved slowly and carefully. If Tom lost his footing or fell, they would all go down together and be swept away by the current toward the village below. But the other two had every confidence in Tom, and Tom had not the slightest reason to doubt himself. They looked like three beavers, moving silently across the current—three heads with three bundles and a little wake of ripples trailing out behind them. Last of all came Nero, the farm dog, paddling faithfully behind them. But Hetty was already out of sight.

Presently there was solid riverbed beneath their feet again. The three children scrambled out on the other side, shook themselves as Nero did, and pulled on their dry, wrinkled clothing.

"Hurry up, Caddie," called Tom. "You're always the last to dress."

"So would you be, too, Tom, if you had so many buttons!" protested Caddie. She came out of the bushes struggling with the back of her blue denim dress. Relenting, Tom turned his superior intelligence to the mean task of buttoning her up the back.

"I wish Mother'd let me wear boys' clothes," she complained.

"Huh!" said Warren. "She thinks you're tomboy enough already."

"But they're so much quicker," said Caddie regretfully.

Now that they were dressed, they sped along the river bank in the direction of the smoke. Several Indian canoes were drawn up on shore in the shelter of a little cove and beyond them in a clearing the Indians moved to and fro about a fire. Propped on two logs was the crude framework of a canoe which was already partly covered with birch bark. The smell of birch smoke and hot pitch filled the air. Caddie lifted her head and sniffed. It was perfume to her, as sweet as the perfume of the clover fields. Nero sniffed, too, and growled low in his throat.

The three children stopped at the edge of the clearing and watched. Even friendly Indians commanded fear and respect in those days. A lean dog, with a wolfish look, came forward barking.

He and Nero circled about each other, little ridges of bristling hair along their spines, their tails wagging suspiciously. Suddenly the Indian dog left Nero and came toward Caddie.

"Look!" said Caddie. "It's Indian John's dog." The dog's tail began to wag in a friendlier manner, and Caddie reached out and patted his head.

By this time the Indians had noticed the children. They spoke

among themselves and pointed. Some of them left their work and
came forward.

In all the seven years since the Woodlawns had come from
Boston to live in the big house on the prairie, the Indians had never
got used to seeing them. White men and their children they had
seen often enough, but never such as these, who wore, above their
pale faces, hair the color of flame and sunset. During the first year
the children spent in Wisconsin, the Indians had come from all the
country around to look at them. They had come in groups, crowding into Mrs. Woodlawn's kitchen in their silent moccasins, touching the children's hair and staring. Poor Mrs. Woodlawn, frightened
nearly out of her wits, had fed them bread or beans or whatever she
had on hand, and they had gone away satisfied.

"Johnny, my dear," Mrs. Woodlawn had complained to her husband, "those frightful savages will eat us out of house and home."

"Patience, Harriet," said her husband, "we have enough and to
spare."

"But, Johnny, the way they look at the children's hair frightens
me. They might want a red scalp to hang to their belts."

Caddie remembered very vividly the day, three years before,
when she had gone unsuspecting into the store in the village. As she
went in the door, a big Indian had seized her and held her up in the
air while he took a leisurely look at her hair. She had been so frightened that she had not even cried out, but hung there, wriggling in
the Indian's firm grasp, and gazing desperately about the store for
help.

The storekeeper had laughed at her, saying in a reassuring
voice: "You needn't be afraid, Caddie. He's a good Indian. It's Indian John."

That was the strange beginning of a friendship, for a kind of
friendship it was, that had grown between Caddie and Indian John.
The boys liked Indian John, too, but it was at Caddie and her red-
gold curls that the big Indian looked when he came to the farm, and
it was for Caddie that he left bits of oddly carved wood and once a

doll–such a funny doll with a tiny head made of a pebble covered with calico, black horsehair braids, calico arms and legs, and a buckskin dress! John's dog knew his master's friends. Caddie had been kind to him and he accepted her as a friend.

He rubbed his head against her now as she patted his rough hair. Indian John left his work on the canoe and came forward.

"You like him dog?" he said, grinning. He was flattered when anyone patted his dog.

"Yes," said Caddie, "he's a good dog."

"Will you let us see how you put the canoe together?" asked Tom eagerly.

"You come look," said the Indian.

They followed him to the half-finished canoe. Grunting and grinning, the Indians took up their work. They fastened the pliable sheaths of birch bark into place on the light framework, first sewing them together with buckskin thongs, then cementing them with the hot pitch. The children were fascinated. Their own canoe on the lake was an Indian canoe. But it had been hollowed out of a single log. They had seen the birch-bark canoes on the river, but had never been so close to the making of one. They were so intent on every detail that time slipped by unheeded. Even the squaws, who came up behind them to examine their hair, did not take their attention from the building of the canoe. Caddie shook her head impatiently, flicking her curls out of their curious fingers, and went on watching.

But after a while Warren said: "Golly! I'm hungry." Perhaps it was the odor of jerked venison, simmering over the fire, which had begun to mingle with the odors of birch and pitch, that made Warren remember he was hungry.

"You're always hungry," said Tom, the lofty one, in a tone of disgust.

"Well, I am, too," said Caddie positively, and that settled it. The sun was beginning to swing low in the sky, and, once they had made up their minds, they were off at once. As quickly as they had come, they returned along the river bank to their crossing place. The Indians stared after them. They did not understand these curious red and white children of the white man, nor how they went and came.

Soon three bundles, three dirty faces, and three fiery heads, shining in the red autumn sun, crossed the river with a little trail of ripples behind them. Safe on the other bank, the three hastily pulled on their clothes and started to take a short cut through the woods, Nero trotting at their heels.

"Hetty probably told Mother, and Mother may be mad at us for going across the river without asking her," said Tom, beginning to turn his thoughts toward home.

"She never said we couldn't," protested Warren.

"Well, maybe she hadn't thought of such a good way of getting across," said Tom, doubtfully.

"Look!" said Caddie. She had stopped beside some hazel brush and was gazing at it with clasped hands. "Nuts! They're ready to pick."

"They're green," said Warren.

"No, they're just right to pick now, if we spread them on the woodshed roof to dry," said Tom judicially. "But we haven't much time." He began to fill his pockets. The others followed his example—only Caddie, who had no pockets, caught up the edges of her skirt and made a bag of that. The boys' pockets were soon filled.

"Come on," said Tom, "we've got enough." But Caddie's skirt was not half filled, and she didn't want to go. Warren was thinking of supper and Tom was remembering that he was the eldest of the three, and that the longer they were gone, the more time his mother would have in which to get angry.

"All right for you," he said, "I'm going home and you'd better come, too." Crackling and rustling through the dry leaves and underbrush, the boys went home. Tom whistled to Nero, but Nero pretended not to hear, for Caddie was his favorite.

Caddie picked furiously, filling her skirt. It was not often that she got more nuts than Tom. Today she would have more than any-body. An evening stillness crept through the golden woods. Sud-denly Caddie knew that she had better go or supper would be begun. To be late for a meal was one of the unpardonable sins in the Woodlawn family. Clutching the edges of her heavy skirt, she began to run. A thorn reached out and tore her sleeve, twigs caught in her tangled hair, her face was dirty and streaked with perspiration, but she didn't stop running until she reached the farmhouse. In fact, she didn't stop even then, for the deserted look of the yard told her that they were all at supper. She rushed on, red and disheveled, and flung open the dining-room door.

There she stopped for the first time, frozen with astonishment and dismay. It wasn't an ordinary supper. It was a company supper! Everybody was calm and clean and sedate, and at one end of the table sat the circuit rider! Paralyzed with horror, Caddie's fingers let go her skirt, and a flood of green hazelnuts rolled all over the floor. In a terrible lull in the conversation they could be heard bumping and rattling to the farthest corners of the room.

THE CIRCUIT RIDER

"How do you do, Caroline Augusta?" said the circuit rider in his deep voice—that voice which filled the schoolhouse with the fervor of his playing. The circuit rider was the only person who bothered to remember that Caddie was really Caroline Augusta and that Hetty was Henrietta. He turned his dark, deep-set eyes on Mrs. Woodlawn, who sat beside him at the end of the long table.

"When are you going to begin making a young lady out of this wild Indian, Mrs. Woodlawn?" he inquired.

The cameo brooch, which she wore only on Sundays or special occasions, rose and fell on Mrs. Woodlawn's bosom. The cameo earrings trembled in her ears, but she answered in as calm a voice as she could muster.

"You must ask my husband that question, Mr. Tanner."

"Caddie!" said Mr. Woodlawn abruptly. "Don't stand there staring, my child. Get washed and to table." Caddie disappeared in an instant. But, as she went, she heard her father saying: "Yes, Mr. Tanner, it is my fault that Caddie is running wild instead of making samplers and dipping candles. I will tell you why."

Caddie heard no more, but she knew what Father had to say. She loved to hear him say it in his deep, quiet voice. He would be telling how frail she and little Mary had been when they came to Wisconsin from Boston, and how, after little Mary had died, he had begged his wife to let him try an experiment with Caddie. "Harriet," he had said, "I want you to let Caddie run wild with the boys. Don't keep her in the house learning to be a lady. I would rather see her learn to plow than make samplers, if she can get her health by doing so. I believe it is worth trying. Bring the other girls up as you like, but let me have Caddie."

So, for seven years, Caddie had run the woods with Tom and Warren. She was no longer pale or delicate. She was brown and strong, and, if Tom climbed a tree, Caddie climbed a taller one. If Warren caught a snake, Caddie went after a longer one. Her mother and sisters looked at her and sighed, but Father smiled and knew that he had been a good doctor.

As these things went through her mind, Caddie ran a comb through her tangled curls and splashed water over her red, dusty face. A few moments later, when she slipped silently into her place between Tom and Warren, the grownups were talking of something else and no one paid any attention to her.

Tom and Warren, still a little untidy and flushed from the afternoon's escapade, glanced at her mischievously. They had come through the barn and seen the circuit rider's horse munching oats in the extra stall. Hastily they had cleaned themselves at the pump and got to the supper table in the very nick of time. Across the table Clara, Hetty, and little Minnie, in white aprons and neat braids, sat up straight and clean with their eyes fixed piously on the circuit rider's face. Even baby Joe, in his high chair, trying his new tooth on a silver spoon, was in spotless white. Mrs. Conroy, the hired girl, moved about the table with fresh supplies of food. Her eyes rested on Caddie in silent amusement. Caddie was her favorite among the Woodlawn children, largely because of the amusing scrapes the child got herself into. Mr. Woodlawn sent a heaping plate of beans and brown bread down to his second daughter, and Caddie ate obediently. But she was smarting with disgrace. Beneath the table, she could still feel some of her hazelnuts rolling about under her feet. And the circuit rider had asked Mother when she intended making a young lady out of her! A young lady, indeed! Who wanted to be a young lady? Certainly not Caddie! But still there were times when it was uncomfortable *not* to be one, even with Father's loyal support.

Misty of Chincoteague

Marguerite Henry

—•❖ Newbery Honor, 1948 ❖•—

On an island off the coasts of Virginia and Maryland lives a band of wild ponies. Among them is Phantom, a rarely seen mare, and her foal, Misty. This is the story of how a sister and a brother come to know these ponies.

Sacred Bones

"Hall-oo-oo!" came a voice down the beach. The boy and the girl turned to see Grandpa Beebe swinging toward them, his gnarled arms upraised like a wind-twisted tree.

"Paul!" he boomed. "Put down that bone. Put it down, I tell ye!"

Paul had forgotten all about the curved piece of wood. Now he noticed that he was clenching it so tightly it left a white streak in the palm of his hand. He dropped it quickly as Grandpa came up.

"How often do I got to tell you that bones is sacred? Even ship's bones."

"Is it true, Grandpa?" asked Paul.

"Be what true?" Grandpa repeated, pulling off his battered felt hat and letting the wind toss his hair.

"About the Spanish galleon being wrecked . . ."

"And the ponies swimming ashore?" added Maureen.

Grandpa Beebe squinted at the sun. "It's nigh onto noontide," he said, "and your Grandma is having sixteen head to dinner tomorrow. We got to get back home to Chincoteague right smart quick! I promised to kill some turkeys for her." He sighed heavily. "Seems as if the devil is allus sittin' cross-legged of me."

But he made no move to go. Instead, he squatted down on the beach, muttering, "Don't see why she's got to parboil 'em today." Then he took off his boots and socks and dug his toes in the sand, like fiddler crabs scuttling for home.

"Feels good, don't it?" he said, with a grin. He looked from Paul to Maureen and back again. "Yer know," he went on, and he began to rub the bristles of his ear, as he always did when he was happy. "Yer know, the best thing about havin' fourteen head of children is ye're bound to get one or two good grandchildren outen the lot."

"Grandpa!" reminded Paul. "Is it true about the Spanish galleon and the ponies? Or is it a legend like the folks over on the mainland say?"

"'Course it's true!" replied Grandpa, with a little show of irritation. "All the wild herds on Assateague be descendants of a bunch of Spanish horses. They wasn't wild to begin with, mind ye. They just went wild with their freedom."

Maureen did a quick little leap, like a colt bucking.

"Then it's *not* a legend?" she rejoiced. "It's *not* a legend!"

"Who said 'twasn't a legend?" Grandpa exclaimed. "'Course it's a legend. But legends be the only stories as is true!"

He stopped to find the right words. "Facts are fine, fer as they go," he said, "but they're like water bugs skittering atop the water. Legends, now—they go deep down and bring up the heart of a story." Here Grandpa shoved his hand into the pocket of his overalls and produced a long stick of licorice and a plug of tobacco. With a pair of wire clippers he divided the licorice in half and gave a piece to Maureen and one to Paul. Then he cut himself a quid of tobacco.

There was a little silence while the old man and the boy and the girl thought about the shipwrecked ponies.

Then, almost in the same breath, Paul and Maureen blurted out together: "Who discovered 'em?"

Grandpa spat out to sea. "Why, I heard tell 'twas the Indians chanced on 'em first. They comes over to hunt on Assateague, and 'twasn't only deer and otter and beaver they finds. They finds these wild ponies pawin' the air and snortin' through their noses, and they ain't never seed no critters like that, blowin' steam and screamin' and their tails and manes a-flyin'. And the Indians was so affrighted they run for their canoes."

Grandpa Beebe began rubbing both ears in his excitement.

"Then what, Grandpa?"

"Why, the ponies was left to run wilder and wilder. Nobody lived here to hinder 'em none, nobody at all. White men come to live on our Chincoteague Island, but Assateague was left to the critters."

Grandpa reached for one of his socks, then broke out in sudden laughter. "Ho! Ho! Ho!" he bellowed.

Paul and Maureen looked all around them. "What's so funny, Grandpa?" they asked.

Grandpa was slapping his thigh, rocking back and forth. "I jes' now thought of somethin' right smart cute," he chuckled, when he could get his breath. "Y'see, lots of folks like to call theirselves descendants of the First Families of Virginia. They kinda makes a high-falutin' club outen it and labels it F.F.V. But you know what?" Here Grandpa's eyes twinkled like the sea with the sun blazing on it.

"What?" chorused Paul and Maureen.

"The real first families of Virginia was the ponies! Ho-ho-ho! That's what *my* history book says!"

"Whee! Grandpa!" exclaimed Paul. "I like the way you talk about history."

Grandpa winked in agreement. "Nothin' so exciting as tag ends pulled right outen the core of the past."

"Did the first white men tame the ponies?" asked Maureen.

"No indeed. Them first white men had no use fer the wild, thrashin' ponies. A slow-going pair o' oxen could do all the plowin' for bread corn and sech. Guess mebee it was Bob Watson's boy of Chincoteague who fust tried to put a wild pony to plow. She was a dead ringer for the Phantom, too. But that was a long time agone."

Paul's heart turned a somersault.

"What happened to her, Grandpa? Did she gentle?"

"Did she gentle! Why, she jes' broke the singletree as if 'twas a matchstick, cleared the fence, and blew to her island home with the reins a-stringin' out behind her."

"Oh!"

"Some of 'em you jest can't gentle. Not after they've lived wild. Only the youngsters is worth botherin' about, so far as the gentlin' goes. Recommember that!"

Paul and Maureen looked at each other. They were thinking of their secret plan to own the Phantom.

Grandpa Beebe began putting on his socks and shoes. "Likely the game warden is done checkin' up on the wild birds. I promised to meet him at Tom's Cove afore the tide ebbs bare. But," he added, as he pulled on his boots, "I know my tides, and I'll give ye time for one more question."

Maureen looked to Paul. "You ask, Paul."

Paul jumped to his feet. How could he ask just one question when dozens popped into his mind? He began picking up fiddler crabs furiously, as if that would help him think. Finally he turned to Grandpa.

"It's about Pony Penning Day," he blurted out. "How did it start?"

It was plain to see that Grandpa Beebe liked the question. He began rubbing the bristles of one ear and then the other. "'Twas this-a-way," he said. "In the yesterdays, when their corn was laid by, folks on Chincoteague got to yearnin' fer a big hollerday. So they sails over to Assateague and rounds up all the wild ponies. 'Twas big sport."

"Like hunting buffalo or deer?" asked Paul.

"'Zactly like that! Only they didn't kill the ponies; just rounded 'em up for the fun of the chase. Then they cut out a few of the younglings to gentle, tried some ropin' and rough ridin' of the wild ones, et a big dinner of outdoor pot pie, and comes on back home to Chincoteague. By-'n-by, they adds somethin' to the fun. They swum the ponies acrost the channel to Chincoteague and put on a big show. 'Twas so excitin', folks come from as far as New York to see it. And afore we knowed it, we was sellin' off some of the colts to the mainlanders."

"Why did they sell the wild things?" asked Maureen.

"Why!" echoed Grandpa. "Why, ponies was overrunnin' Assateague. They was gettin' thick as raisins in a pie!"

"That thick, Grandpa?" asked Maureen, her eyes rounded.

"Maybe not that thick," grinned Grandpa.

"Don't keep interrupting Grandpa!" exclaimed Paul.

"Today it's jest the same," Grandpa said slowly. "Along toward the tail end of July, when the ponies is done with fightin' and foalin' and the watermen is tired of plantin' oysters, then we all get to hankerin' for a celebration. So the menfolk round up the ponies, the womenfolk bake meat pot pie, and there ye are! Only now, outside a few hossmen like me, the fire department owns most of the wild ponies. And a good thing it is for Chincoteague."

"Why is it?"

"'Cause all the money they make from sellin' 'em goes into our fire-fightin' apparatus."

Grandpa Beebe rose stiffly. "Come on, you two, I hain't got time to school ye. That's what me and Grandma pays taxes for. Besides, we been a-settin' here so long the sand is liable to drift up over us and make another white clift outen us. It's time we was gettin' back home to Chincoteague, and Grandma's turkeys."

A PIECE OF WIND AND SKY

April, May, June, July! Only four months until Pony Penning Day. Only four months to plan and work for the Phantom.

Suddenly Time was important.

"We got to lay a course and hold it," said Paul, as he whisked over the fence that same afternoon and began studying the ponies in Grandpa Beebe's corral.

Maureen slipped between the rails and caught up with him. "Quit talking like a waterman, Paul. Talk like a horseman so I can understand you."

"All right, I will. Grandpa's got eleven mares here. Six of 'em have a colt apiece, and the black and the chestnut each have a yearling and a suckling. Between now and July, how many colts do you reckon Grandpa will sell?"

"Probably all of 'em—except the sucklings, of course."

"That's what I figure! Now if we could halter-break the colts and teach 'em some manners, folks'd pay more for them, wouldn't they?"

"I reckon."

"All right!" exclaimed Paul as he sailed back over the fence. "Maybe Grandpa will pay us the difference."

That night at the supper table Paul looked up over his plate of roast oysters and caught Grandma's eye.

"Grandma," he questioned, "do you like a mannerly colt?"

Grandma Beebe's face was round as a holly berry and soft little whiskers grew about her mouth, like the feelers of a very young colt. She pursed her lips now, wondering if there were some catch to Paul's question.

"Paul means," explained Maureen, "if you came here to Pony Ranch to buy a colt, would you choose one that was gentled or would you choose a wild one?"

Grandpa chuckled. "Can't you jes' see yer Grandma crowhoppin' along on a wild colt!"

"That's yer answer," laughed Grandma, as she cut golden squares of cornbread. "I'd take the mannerly colt."

Paul swallowed a plump oyster, almost choking in his haste. "Would you," he gulped, "that is, would you be willing to pay out more money for it, Grandma?"

"Wa-al, that depends," mused Grandma, passing the breadboard around, "that depends on how *much* more."

"Would you pay ten dollars more?"

"If he was nice and mannerly, I would. Yes, I would."

"See there, Grandpa!" The words came out in a rush. "If Maureen and I was to halter-break the colts, could we–" He stopped, and then stammered, "Could we have the ten extra dollars for each colt sold?"

So dead a silence fell over the table that the *drip-drip* of the kitchen faucet sounded like hammer strokes.

Grandpa slowly buttered his bread and then glanced about the table.

"Pass your Grandpa the goody, Maureen."

All eyes watched Grandpa spread a layer of wild blackberry jam on top of the butter. Then he added another square of cornbread to make a sandwich. Not until he had tasted and approved did he turn to Paul.

"What fer?" he barked.

Paul and Maureen stared at their plates.

"Must be a secret, Clarence," Grandma pleaded.

Grandpa swept a few crumbs into his hand and began stacking his own dishes. "I ain't never pried a secret outa no one," he said. "And I don't aim to start pokin' and pryin' now. It's a deal, children, and ye don't need to tell me what the money's fer until ye're ready to spend it."

Paul and Maureen flew to Grandpa and hugged him. For a moment they forgot that they were almost grown up.

The days and weeks that followed were not half long enough. Up at dawn, working with the colts, haltering them, teaching them to lead and to stand tied! Going to school regretfully and hurrying home as soon as it was out!

Now when a buyer came to look at the colts, Maureen did not run to her room as she used to do, pressing her face in the feather bed to stifle her sobs. Nor did Paul swing up on one of Grandpa's ponies and gallop down the hard point of land to keep from crying. Now they actually led the colts out to the buyers to show how gentle they were. They even helped load them onto waiting trucks. All the while they kept thinking that soon they would have a pony of their own, never to be sold. *Not for any price.*

April and May passed. School closed.

Paul and Maureen worked furiously for the Phantom. They caught and sold crabs. They gathered oysters when the tide went out and laid the oyster rocks bare. And most exciting of all, they "treaded for clams." In flannel moccasins to protect their feet, and wide-brimmed hats on their heads, they plunged into Chincoteague Bay. Sometimes they would whinny and snort, pretending they were wild ponies escaping the flies. Then suddenly they would feel the thin edge of a clam with their feet and remember that they were clam treaders, trying to earn money for the Phantom.

Paul learned how to burrow under the sand with his toes and lift the clam to the surface on the top of his moccasined foot. But try as she would, Maureen never could do it. She raked the clams instead, with a long wooden rake. Then she dumped them into a home-made basket formed by spreading a piece of canvas inside an old inner tube. She kept it from floating out to sea by tying it to her waist with a rope.

Slowly, week by week, Grandpa's old tobacco pouch in which they stored their money began to round out, until it held exactly one hundred dollars. It never occurred to Paul and Maureen that the Phantom might escape the roundup men this year, too. They felt as certain of owning her as if someone had sent them a telegram that read,

SHIPPING YOUR PONY ON PONY PENNING DAY

One early morning, when July was coming in, Paul cornered Grandpa hustling across the barnyard. He stepped right into Grandpa's path so that he had to stop short.

"Grandpa!" Paul burst out. "Will you rent me one of your empty stalls beginning with Pony Penning Day? I'll do a man's work to pay for it."

Grandpa roughed his hand up the back of Paul's head. "Who you want it fer, lad? Plan to sleep in it yourself?"

Paul's face turned red. "I," he hesitated. "That is, Maureen and I are going to . . ."

"Wa-al?"

"We're going to buy—we're going to buy the Phantom on Pony Penning Day."

There! The news was out!

Grandpa threw back his head. He opened wide his mouth, ready to break out in laughter, but when he saw the grave look in Paul's eyes, he did not laugh at all. Instead, he let out a shrill "Wee-dee-dee-dee, wee-dee-dee-dee," as he pulled a handful of corn out of his pocket and spattered the golden kernels about his feet.

From all over the barnyard came wild geese and tame geese, big ducks and little ducks, marsh hens and chicks. The air was wild with the clatter they made.

"Can't no one catch the Phantom," Grandpa yelled above the noise. "For two years she's give the horse laugh to the best roundup men we got on Chincoteague. What makes ye think she's going to *ask* to be caught?"

"Because," Paul shouted through the din, "because the Fire Chief promised I could go along this year."

Grandpa Beebe stepped back a pace and studied his grandson. His clear eyes twinkled with merriment. Then a look of pity crossed his face.

"Lad," he said, "the Phantom don't wear that white map on her withers for nothing. It stands for Liberty, and ain't no human being going to take her liberty away from her."

"She wants to come to us," Paul said, trying to keep his voice steady. "Ever since that day on Assateague, Maureen and I knew."

A white striker bird flew up from the ground and perched on Grandpa's gnarled forefinger. Grandpa directed his remarks to the bird. "Can't fer the life of me see why those two want another pony. Why, the corral's full of 'em. They're as much Paul's and Maureen's as anybody's."

Paul's lips tightened. "It's not the same," he said. "Owning a pony you never have to sell . . ."

The striker bird flew away. Paul and Grandpa watched in silence as it dipped and rose to the sky.

Grandpa stood in thought. "Paul boy," he said slowly, "hark to my words. The Phantom ain't a hoss. She ain't even a lady. She's just a piece of wind and sky."

Paul tried to speak, swallowed, and tried once more. "We got our hearts set on her," he faltered.

Grandpa pushed his battered hat to one side and scratched his head. "All right, boy," he sighed. "The stall is yours."

A moment later Paul was telling Maureen the good news. "Owning a stall is next best to owning a pony," she laughed, as they both went to work in a fever of excitement.

With long brooms and steaming pails of water, they washed the walls and the ceiling of Phantom's stall. They scraped inches of sand from the hard-packed floor, dumped it in the woods, and brought in fresh, clean sand. They built a manger, spending long moments deciding just how high it should be placed. They scrubbed a rain barrel to be used for a watering trough. They even dug a "wickie"–the long, tough root of a brier that trails along under the ground.

"Phantom won't be frightened when she smells and feels a wickie halter," Maureen said. "It'll be much softer than rope."

The Courage of Sarah Noble

Alice Dalgliesh

—:• NEWBERY HONOR, 1955 •:—

IN 1707, EIGHT-YEAR-OLD SARAH NOBLE FINDS THE COURAGE TO TRAVEL WITH HER FATHER TO THE CONNECTICUT WILDERNESS TO BUILD A NEW HOME FOR THEIR FAMILY.

NIGHT IN THE FOREST

Sarah lay on a quilt under a tree. The darkness was all around her, but through the branches she could see one bright star. It was comfortable to look at.

The spring night was cold, and Sarah drew her warm cloak close. That was comfortable, too. She thought of how her mother had put it around her the day she and her father started out on this long, hard journey.

"Keep up your courage," her mother had said, fastening the cloak under Sarah's chin. "Keep up your courage, Sarah Noble!"

And, indeed, Sarah needed to keep up her courage, for she and her father were going all the way into the wilderness of Connecticut to build a house.

This was the first night they had spent in the forest—the other nights they had come to a settlement. Thomas, the brown horse, was tied nearby. He was asleep on his feet. Against a tree Sarah's father sat, his musket across his knees. Sometimes he nodded, but Sarah knew that if she called to him he would wake. Suddenly she had a great need to hear his voice, even though she could not see his face.

"Wooo-oooh!" Such a strange sound from a nearby tree.

"Father?"

"An owl, Sarah. He is telling you goodnight."

Another louder, longer sound, a stranger sound, as if someone were in pain.

"Father?"

"A fox, Sarah. He is no bigger than a dog. He is calling to his mate."

Sarah closed her eyes and tried to sleep. Then came a sound that made her open her eyes and sit right up.

"FATHER!"

"Yes, Sarah, it is a wolf. But I have my musket, and I am awake."

"I can't sleep, Father. Tell me about home?"

"What shall I tell you, Sarah?"

"Anything—if it is about home."

Now the howl of the wolf was a little farther away.

"You remember how it was, Sarah, the day I came home to tell of the land I had bought? You were rocking the baby in the cradle . . ."

"And the baby would not sleep."

"And your mother said . . ."

"You know I cannot take the baby on a long journey. She is so young and she is not strong."

Sarah could see her worried little mother, bending over the cradle, clucking and fussing like a mother hen.

The wolf was farther away, but still one could hear it.

"And you said . . ."

"I said, 'I will go and cook for you, Father.'"

"It was a blessing the Lord gave me daughters, as well as sons," said John Noble. "And one of them all of eight years old, and a born cook. For Mary would not come, nor Hannah."

"No," said Sarah, her voice sounding a little sleepy. "Hannah–would–not–come–nor Mary. It is good–I–like–to cook."

But she felt suddenly and terribly lonely for her mother and for the big family of brothers and sisters. John . . . David . . . Stephen . . . Mary . . . Hannah . . . three-year-old Margaret . . . the baby . . . And–*could* she really cook? She had never made a pie. But–maybe–you–don't–need–pies–in–the–wilderness. Keep–up–your–courage–Sarah–Noble. Keep–up . . . And holding tightly to a fold of the warm cloak, Sarah was asleep.

Now the wolf was very far away. But Thomas, who had raised his head when he heard it, still stood with his ears lifted . . . listening.

And Sarah's father sat there, wondering if he should have brought this child into the wilderness. When the first light of morning came through the trees, he was still awake.

Night in the Settlement

The next night was quite different. They came at sundown to a settlement. The houses were brown and homelike. In two of them the sticks of pine used instead of candles were already burning. They shone through the windows with a warm golden light that seemed to say, "Welcome, Sarah Noble!"

Sarah, riding on Thomas, looked down at her father, walking beside her. It had been a long day, and the trail through the forest had not been easy.

"We will spend the night here, Father?"

"Yes," said her father. "And you will sleep safely in a warm house."

Sarah sighed with pleasure. "Lift me down and let me walk, Father? Poor Thomas carries so much he should not carry me too far."

So they were walking, all three of them, when they came to the cabin where the candle wood was lighted early.

They knocked. The latch was lifted and a woman stood in the doorway looking at them.

She is not like my mother, Sarah thought. *Her face is not like a mother's face.*

Still the woman stood and looked at them.

"Good evening," Sarah's father said. "I am John Noble from the Massachusetts colony, and this is my daughter, Sarah. We are on our way to New Milford where I have bought land to build a house. Can you tell us where we could put up for the night?"

The woman looked at them, still without smiling.

"We have not much room," she said, "but you may share what we have. My husband, Andrew Robinson, is away . . . and I had thought it might be wandering Indians. If you do not mind sleeping by the fire . . ."

"We slept in the forest last night," John Noble said. "Anything under a roof will seem fine to us."

So they went in, and Sarah saw the children who were in the house. There were four of them, two boys and two girls, all staring at Sarah with big round eyes. She began to feel shy. And now she was alone, for her father had gone to see to Thomas, and to bring in Sarah's quilt for her to sleep on.

"Be seated," said Mistress Robinson. "You are welcome to share what we have. Lemuel, Abigail, Robert, Mary, this is Sarah Noble."

Sarah smiled timidly at the children.

"Take off your cloak, Sarah."

But Sarah held it closely. "If you do not mind," she said, "I will keep it–I am–I am a little cold."

The children laughed. Sarah sat down at the table, and in a few minutes her father was with them. Now Sarah let the cloak fall back from her shoulders.

"I will hang it up for you," said Abigail. "It is a beautiful warm cloak." Her fingers stroked the cloak lovingly as she hung it on a peg.

"And it is a kind of red," she said. "I would like to have a new cloak."

"You have no need of a new cloak," said her mother, sharply.

Now Mistress Robinson began to ask questions. And as John Noble answered, she began clucking and fussing just as Sarah's mother might have done. But somehow Sarah's mother fussed in a loving way.

"Taking this dear child into the wilderness with those heathen savages. . . . And she not more than seven. . . ."

"Eight," said Sarah, "though my mother says I am not tall for my age."

"Eight then—what will you do there all alone?"

"My father is with me," Sarah said.

The children's eyes had grown wider and rounder. Now they began to laugh and the younger ones pointed at Sarah.

"She is going to live away off in the woods."

"The Indians will eat you," Lemuel said and smacked his lips loudly.

"They will chop off your head," little Robert added, with an innocent smile.

"They will not hurt me," Sarah said. "My father says the Indians are friendly."

"I have heard that they are friendly," Mistress Robinson put in quickly. "The men who bought the land gave them a fair price."

"And promised they might keep their right to fish in the Great River," said John Noble.

"They will chop off your head," said Robert, and made chopping motions with his hand.

Sarah felt a little sick. This was worse than wolves in the night. Her brothers were not like these boys—and she had heard about Indians. Perhaps . . . perhaps these Indians had changed their minds about being friendly.

She was glad when the children went to bed–all except Abigail, who spoke gently.

"Don't mind the boys," Abigail whispered. "They tease."

But Sarah did mind. If Stephen were with them these boys would not dare to tease her, she thought.

At last it was quiet. The children were all in bed, and Sarah lay on her quilt by the fire. Mistress Robinson covered her up warmly, and for a moment she seemed a little like Sarah's mother.

Then: "So young, so young," she said. "A great pity."

"I would like to have my cloak, if you please," said Sarah.

"But you are warm . . ."

"I am a little cold . . . now."

Mistress Robinson put the cloak over Sarah. "Have it your way, child. But your blood must be thin."

Sarah caught a fold of the cloak in her hand and held it tightly. As she closed her eyes she could see pictures against the dark. They were not comfortable pictures. Before her were miles and miles of trees. Trees, dark and fearful, trees crowding against each other, trees on and on, more trees and more trees. Behind the trees there were men moving . . . were they Indians?

She held the warm material of the cloak even more closely.

"Keep up your courage, Sarah Noble. Keep up your courage!" she whispered to herself.

But it was quite a long time before she slept.

DOWN THE LONG HILL

Now they had come to the last day of the journey. The Indian trail had been narrow, the hills went up and down, up and down. Sarah and her father were tired, and even Thomas walked wearily.

By late afternoon they would be home. Home? No, it wasn't really home, just a place out in the wilderness. But after a while it would be home, John Noble told Sarah it would be. His voice kept leading her on.

"Now we must be about two miles away."

"Now it is surely a mile . . . only a mile."

Sarah's tired feet seemed to dance. She picked some wild flowers and stuck them in the harness behind Thomas's ear.

"You must be well dressed, Thomas," she said. "We are coming home."

She put a pink flower on her own dress and her feet danced along again. Then suddenly she stopped.

"Father, if there is no house where shall we live?"

Her father smiled down at her. "I have told you . . ."

"Then tell me again. I like to hear."

"I hope to find a cave in the side of a hill," he said. "I will make a hut for us, and a fence around it. Then you and Thomas and I will live there until the house is built. Though Thomas will have to help me with the building."

Sarah laughed. "Thomas cannot build a house!" She had a funny picture in her mind of solemn, long-faced Thomas carefully putting the logs in place.

"He can drag logs," her father said. "Soon we shall have a fine house like Mistress Robinson's."

"No," said Sarah. "Like our own."

"And why not like Mistress Robinson's?"

"Because there is no love in that house," said Sarah.

"You are too wise for your years," her father told her.

Now they had come to the top of a long, steep hill and they stopped at a place where there were not many trees, only bushes and coarse grass.

"This is one of the bare places," John Noble said. "The Indians have cleared it for a hunting ground."

Sarah looked around her fearfully. Behind the bushes something stirred . . .

"A deer," said her father, and raised his gun. But Sarah clung to him.

"No, Father, no! Do not shoot it!"

"But we must have meat . . ."

"Not now, not now," Sarah begged. "Its eyes are so gentle, Father."

"Well . . ." said John Noble. But he did not shoot.

The deer rushed away, its white tail showing like a flag. Then Sarah drew a long breath and looked down.

Below there was a valley. "And you would see the Great River if it were not for the trees," her father said.

Sarah looked and looked and filled her mind with the beauty of it. It was a beauty that would stay with her all her life. Beyond the valley there were green hills, and beyond . . . and beyond . . . and beyond . . . more hills of a strange, soft and misty blue.

The trees were the dark green of firs and the light green of birches in springtime. And now they were friendly. They were not like the angry dark trees that had seemed to stand in their path as they came.

"I do like it," Sarah said. "And I do not see any Indians."

"The Indians are by the Great River," her father said. "And I have told you, Sarah, they are good Indians."

"But Lemuel said . . ."

John Noble took Sarah's small, cold hand in his.

"Mistress Robinson should teach her children to watch their words. She should watch her own. And there are people in this world who do not help others along the way, Sarah, while there are those who do. In our home all will be treated with kindness—always, Sarah. The Indians, too, and they will not harm us."

Now Sarah held her courage a little more firmly. She also held tightly to her father's hand. And so they came, with Thomas, down the long hill into the place that would be their home.

From the Mixed-Up Files of Mrs. Basil E. Frankweiler

E. L. Konigsburg

—❖ NEWBERY MEDAL, 1968 ❖—

HAVING RUN AWAY WITH HER YOUNGER BROTHER TO LIVE IN THE METRO-POLITAN MUSEUM OF ART IN NEW YORK CITY, TWELVE-YEAR-OLD CLAUDIA STRIVES TO KEEP THINGS IN ORDER IN THEIR NEW HOME.

To my lawyer, Saxonberg:

I can't say that I enjoyed your last visit. It was obvious that you had too much on your mind to pay any attention to what I was trying to say. Perhaps, if you had some interest in this world besides law, taxes, and your grandchildren, you could almost be a fascinating person. Almost. That last visit was the worst bore. I won't risk another dull visit for a while, so I'm having Sheldon, my chauffeur, deliver this account to your home. I've written it to explain certain changes I want made in my last will and testament. You'll understand those changes (and a lot of other things) much better after reading it. I'm sending you a carbon copy; I'll keep an original in my files. I don't come in until much later, but never mind. You'll find enough to interest you until I do.

You never knew that I could write this well, did you? Of course, you don't actually know yet, but you soon will. I've spent a lot of time on this file. I listened. I investigated, and I fitted all the pieces together like a jigsaw puzzle. It leaves no doubts. Well, Saxonberg, read and discover.

Mrs. Basil E. Frankweiler

As soon as they reached the sidewalk, Jamie made his first decision as treasurer. "We'll walk from here to the museum."

"Walk?" Claudia asked. "Do you realize that it is over forty blocks from here?"

"Well, how much does the bus cost?"

"The bus!" Claudia exclaimed. "Who said anything about taking a bus? I want to take a taxi."

"Claudia," Jamie said, "you are quietly out of your mind. How can you even think about a taxi? We have no more allowance. No more income. You can't be extravagant any longer. It's not my money we're spending. It's *our* money. We're in this together, remember?"

"You're right," Claudia answered. "A taxi is expensive. The bus is cheaper. It's only twenty cents each. We'll take the bus."

"*Only* twenty cents each. That's forty cents total. No bus. We'll walk."

"We'll wear out forty cents worth of shoe leather," Claudia mumbled. "You're sure we have to walk?"

"Positive," Jamie answered. "Which way do we go?"

"Sure you won't change your mind?" The look on Jamie's face gave her the answer. She sighed. No wonder Jamie had more than twenty-four dollars; he was a gambler and a cheapskate. If that's the way he wants to be, she thought, I'll never again ask him for bus fare; I'll suffer and never, never let him know about it. But he'll regret it when I simply collapse from exhaustion. I'll collapse quietly.

"We'd better walk up Madison Avenue," she told her brother. "I'll see too many ways to spend *our* precious money if we walk on Fifth Avenue. All those gorgeous stores."

She and Jamie did not walk exactly side by side. Her violin case kept bumping him, and he began to walk a few steps ahead of her. As Claudia's pace slowed down from what she was sure was an accumulation of carbon dioxide in her system (she had not yet learned about muscle fatigue in science class even though she was in sixth grade honors class), Jamie's pace quickened. Soon he was walking a block and a half ahead of her. They would meet when a red light held him up. At one of these mutual stops Claudia instructed Jamie to wait for her on the corner of Madison Avenue and 80th Street, for there they would turn left to Fifth Avenue.

She found Jamie standing on that corner, probably one of the most civilized street corners in the whole world, consulting a compass and announcing that when they turned left, they would be heading "due northwest." Claudia was tired and cold at the tips; her fingers, her toes, her nose were all cold while the rest of her was perspiring under the weight of her winter clothes. She never liked feeling very hot or very cold, and she hated feeling both at the same time. "Head due northwest. Head due northwest," she mimicked. "Can't you simply say turn right or turn left as everyone else does? Who do you think you are? Daniel Boone? I'll bet no one's used a compass in Manhattan since Henry Hudson."

Jamie didn't answer. He briskly rounded the corner of 80th Street and made his hand into a sun visor as he peered down the street. Claudia needed an argument. Her internal heat, the heat of anger, was cooking that accumulated carbon dioxide. It would soon explode out of her if she didn't give it some vent. "Don't you realize that we must try to be inconspicuous?" she demanded of her brother.

"What's inconspicuous?"

"Un-noticeable."

Jamie looked all around. "I think you're brilliant, Claude. New York is a great place to hide out. No one notices no one."

"Anyone," Claudia corrected. She looked at Jamie and found him smiling. She softened. She had to agree with her brother. She was brilliant. New York was a great place, and being called brilliant had cooled her down. The bubbles dissolved. By the time they reached the museum, she no longer needed an argument.

As they entered the main door on Fifth Avenue, the guard clicked off two numbers on his people counter. Guards always count the people going into the museum, but they don't count them going out. (My chauffeur, Sheldon, has a friend named Morris who is a guard at the Metropolitan. I've kept Sheldon busy getting information from Morris. It's not hard to do since Morris loves to talk about his work. He'll tell about anything except security. Ask him a question he won't or can't answer, and he says, "I'm not at liberty to tell. Security.")

By the time Claudia and Jamie reached their destination, it was one o'clock, and the museum was busy. On any ordinary Wednesday over 26,000 people come. They spread out over the twenty acres of floor space; they roam from room to room to room to room. On Wednesday come the gentle old ladies who are using the time before the Broadway matinee begins. They walk around in pairs. You can tell they are a set because they wear matching pairs of orthopedic shoes, the kind that lace on the side. Tourists visit the museum on Wednesdays. You can tell them because the men carry cameras, and the women look as if their feet hurt; they wear high heeled shoes. (I always say that those who wear 'em deserve 'em.) And there are art students. Any day of the week. They also walk around in pairs. You can tell that they are a set because they carry matching black sketchbooks.

(You've missed all this, Saxonberg. Shame on you! You've never set your well-polished shoe inside that museum. More than a quarter of a million people come to that museum every week. They come from Mankato, Kansas, where they have no museums and from Paris, France, where they have lots. And they all enter free of charge because that's what they museum is: great and large and wonderful and free to all. And complicated. Complicated enough even for Jamie Kincaid.)

No one thought it strange that a boy and a girl, each carrying a book bag and an instrument case and who would normally be in school, were visiting a museum. After all, about a thousand school children visit the museum every day. The guard at the entrance merely stopped them and told them to check their cases and book bags. A museum rule: no bags, food, or umbrellas. None that the guards can see. Rule or no rule, Claudia decided it was a good idea. A big sign in the checking room said NO TIPPING, so she knew that Jamie couldn't object. Jamie did object, however; he pulled his sister aside and asked her how she expected him to change into his pajamas. His pajamas, he explained, were rolled into a tiny ball in his trumpet case.

Claudia told him that she fully expected to check out at 4:30. They would then leave the museum by the front door and within five minutes would re-enter from the back, through the door that leads from the parking lot to the Children's Museum. After all, didn't that solve all their problems? (1) They would be seen leaving the museum. (2) They would be free of their baggage while they scouted around for a place to spend the night. And (3) it was free.

Claudia checked her coat as well as her packages. Jamie was condemned to walking around in his ski jacket. When the jacket was on and zippered, it covered up that exposed strip of skin. Besides, the orlon plush lining did a great deal to muffle his twenty-four-dollar rattle. Claudia would never have permitted herself to become so overheated, but Jamie liked perspiration, a little bit of dirt, and complications.

Right now, however, he wanted lunch. Claudia wished to eat in the restaurant on the main floor, but Jamie wished to eat in the snack bar downstairs; he thought it would be less glamorous, but cheaper, and as chancellor of the exchequer, as holder of the veto power, and as tightwad of the year, he got his wish. Claudia didn't really mind too much when she saw the snack bar. It was plain but clean.

Jamie was dismayed at the prices. They had $28.61 when they went into the cafeteria, and only $27.11 when they came out still feeling hungry. "Claudia," he demanded, "did you know food would cost so much? Now, aren't you glad that we didn't take a bus?"

Claudia was no such thing. She was not glad that they hadn't taken a bus. She was merely furious that her parents, and Jamie's too, had been so stingy that she had been away from home for less than one whole day and was already worried about survival money. She chose not to answer Jamie. Jamie didn't notice; he was completely wrapped up in problems of finance.

"Do you think I could get one of the guards to play me a game of war?" he asked.

"That's ridiculous," Claudia said.

"Why? I brought my cards along. A whole deck."

Claudia said, "*Inconspicuous* is exactly the opposite of that. Even a guard at the Metropolitan who sees thousands of people every day would remember a boy who played him a game of cards."

Jamie's pride was involved. "I cheated Bruce through all second grade and through all third grade so far, and he still isn't wise."

"Jamie! Is that how you knew you'd win?"

Jamie bowed his head and answered, "Well, yeah. Besides, Brucie has trouble keeping straight the jacks, queens, and kings. He gets mixed up."

"Why do you cheat your best friend?"

"I sure don't know. I guess I like complications."

"Well, quit worrying about money now. Worry about where we're going to hide while they're locking up this place."

They took a map from the information stand for free. Claudia selected where they would hide during that dangerous time immediately after the museum was closed to the public and before all the guards and helpers left. She decided that she would go to the ladies' room, and Jamie would go to the men's room just before the museum closed. "Go to the one near the restaurant on the main floor," she told Jamie.

"I'm not spending a night in a men's room. All that tile. It's cold. And, besides, men's rooms make noises sound louder. And I rattle enough now."

Claudia explained to Jamie that he was to enter a booth in the men's room. "And then stand on it," she continued.

"Stand on it? Stand on what?" Jamie demanded.

"You know," Claudia insisted. "Stand on it!"

"You mean stand on the toilet?" Jamie needed everything spelled out.

"Well, what else would I mean? What else is there in a booth in the men's room? And keep your head down. And keep the door to the booth very slightly open," Claudia finished.

"Feet up. Head down. Door open. Why?"

"Because I'm certain that when they check the ladies' room and the men's room, they peek under the door and check only to see if there are feet. We must stay there until we're sure all the people and guards have gone home."

"How about the night watchman?" Jamie asked.

Claudia displayed a lot more confidence than she really felt. "Oh! there'll be a night watchman, I'm sure. But he mostly walks around the roof trying to keep people from breaking in. We'll already be in. They call what he walks, a cat walk. We'll learn his habits soon enough. They must mostly use burglar alarms in the inside. We'll just never touch a window, a door, or a valuable painting. Now, let's find a place to spend the night."

They wandered back to the rooms of fine French and English furniture. It was here Claudia knew for sure that she had chosen the most elegant place in the world to hide. She wanted to sit on the lounge chairs that had been made for Marie Antoinette or at least sit at her writing table. But signs everywhere said not to step on the platform. And some of the chairs had silken ropes strung across the arms to keep you from even trying to sit down. She would have to wait until after lights out to be Marie Antoinette.

At last she found a bed that she considered perfectly wonderful, and she told Jamie that they would spend the night there. The bed had a tall canopy, supported by an ornately carved headboard at one end and by two gigantic posts at the other. (I'm familiar with that bed, Saxonberg. It is as enormous and fussy as mine. And it dates from the sixteenth century like mine. I once considered donating my bed to the museum, but Mr. Untermyer gave them this one first. I was somewhat relieved when he did. Now I can enjoy my bed without feeling guilty because the museum doesn't have one. Besides, I'm not that fond of donating things.)

Claudia had always known that she was meant for such fine things. Jamie, on the other hand, thought that running away from home to sleep in just another bed was really no challenge at all. He, James, would rather sleep on the bathroom floor, after all. Claudia then pulled him around to the foot of the bed and told him to read what the card said.

Jamie read, "Please do not step on the platform."

Claudia knew that he was being difficult on purpose; therefore, she read for him, "State bed–scene of the alleged murder of Amy Robsart, first wife of Lord Robert Dudley, later Earl of . . ."

Jamie couldn't control his smile. He said, "You know, Claude, for a sister and a fussbudget, you're not too bad."

Claudia replied, "You know, Jamie, for a brother and a cheapskate, you're not too bad."

Something happened at precisely that moment. Both Claudia and Jamie tried to explain to me about it, but they couldn't quite. I know what happened, though I never told them. Having words and explanations for everything is too modern. I especially wouldn't tell Claudia. She has too many explanations already.

What happened was: they became a team, a family of two.

There had been times before they ran away when they had acted like a team, but those were very different from *feeling* like a team. Becoming a team didn't mean the end of their arguments. But it did mean that the arguments became a part of the adventure, became discussions not threats. To an outsider the arguments would appear to be the same because feeling like part of a team is something that happens invisibly. You might call it *caring*. You could even call it *love*. And it is very rarely, indeed, that it happens to two people at the same time—especially a brother and a sister who had always spent more time with activities than they had with each other.

They followed their plan: checked out of the museum and re-entered through a back door. When the guard at that entrance told them to check their instrument cases, Claudia told him that they were just passing through on their way to meet their mother. The guard let them go, knowing that if they went very far, some other guard would stop them again. However, they managed to avoid other guards for the remaining minutes until the bell rang. The bell meant that the museum was closing in five minutes. They then entered the booths of the rest rooms.

They waited in the booths until five-thirty, when they felt certain that everyone had gone. Then they came out and met. Five-thirty in winter is dark, but nowhere seems as dark as the Metropolitan Museum of Art. The ceilings are so high that they fill up with a lot of darkness. It seemed to Jamie and Claudia that they walked through miles of corridors. Fortunately, the corridors were wide, and they were spared bumping into things.

At last they came to the hall of the English Renaissance. Jamie quickly threw himself upon the bed forgetting that it was only about six o'clock and thinking that he would be so exhausted that he would immediately fall asleep. He didn't. He was hungry. That was one reason he didn't fall asleep immediately. He was uncomfortable, too. So he got up from bed, changed into his pajamas and got back into bed. He felt a little better. Claudia had already changed into her pajamas. She, too, was hungry, and she, too, was uncomfortable. How could so elegant and romantic a bed smell so musty? She would have liked to wash everything in a good, strong, sweet-smelling detergent.

As Jamie got into bed, he still felt uneasy, and it wasn't because he was worried about being caught. Claudia had planned everything so well that he didn't concern himself about that. The strange way he felt had little to do with the strange place in which they were sleeping. Claudia felt it, too. Jamie lay there thinking. Finally, realization came.

"You know, Claude," he whispered, "I didn't brush my teeth."

Claudia answered, "Well, Jamie, you can't always brush after every meal." They both laughed very quietly. "Tomorrow," Claudia reassured him, "we'll be even better organized."

It was much earlier than her bedtime at home, but still Claudia felt tired. She thought she might have an iron deficiency anemia: tired blood. Perhaps, the pressures of everyday stress and strain had gotten her down. Maybe she was light-headed from hunger; her brain cells were being robbed of vitally needed oxygen for good growth and, and . . . yawn.

She shouldn't have worried. It had been an unusually busy day. A busy and unusual day. So she lay there in the great quiet of the museum next to the warm quiet of her brother and allowed the soft stillness to settle around them: a comforter of quiet. The silence seeped from their heads to their soles and into their souls. They stretched out and relaxed. Instead of oxygen and stress, Claudia thought now of hushed and quiet words: glide, fur, banana, peace. Even the footsteps of the night watchman added only an accented quarter-note to the silence that had become a hum, a lullaby.

They lay perfectly still even long after he passed. Then they whispered good night to each other and fell asleep. They were quiet sleepers and hidden by the heaviness of the dark, they were easily not discovered.

(Of course, Saxonberg, the draperies of that bed helped, too.)

Jennifer, Hecate, Macbeth, William McKinley, and Me, Elizabeth

E. L. Konigsburg

—⁑ Newbery Honor, 1968 ⁑—

In this story set in New York, fifth-grader Elizabeth is the loneliest child in the whole U. S. of A—until she meets Jennifer, who claims to be a witch.

I first met Jennifer on my way to school. It was Halloween, and she was sitting in a tree. I was going back to school from lunch. This particular lunch hour was only a little different from usual because of Halloween. We were told to dress in costume for the school Halloween parade. I was dressed as a Pilgrim.

I always walked the back road to school, and I always walked alone. We had moved to the apartment house in town in September just before school started, and I walked alone because I didn't have anyone to walk with. I walked the back way because it passed through a little woods that I liked. Jennifer was sitting in one of the trees in this woods.

Our apartment house had grown on a farm about ten years before. There was still a small farm across the street; it included a big white house, a greenhouse, a caretaker's house, and a pump painted green without a handle. The greenhouse had clean windows; they shone in the sun. I could see only the roof windows from our second floor apartment. The rest were hidden by trees and shrubs. My mother never called the place a farm; she always called it THE ESTATE. It was old; the lady who owned it was old. She had given part of her land to the town for a park, and the town named the park after her: Samellson Park. THE ESTATE gave us a beautiful view from our apartment. My mother liked trees.

Our new town was not full of apartments. Almost everyone else lived in houses. There were only three apartment buildings as big as ours. All three sat on the top of the hill from the train station. Hundreds of men rode the train to New York City every morning and rode it home every night. My father did. In the mornings the elevators would be full of kids going to school and fathers going to the train. The kids left the building by the back door and ran down one side of the hill to the school. The fathers left the building by the front door and ran down the other side of the hill to the station.

Other kids from the apartment chose to walk to school through the little woods. The footsteps of all of them for ten years had worn away the soil so that the roots of the trees were bare and made steps for walking up and down the steep slope. The little woods made better company than the sidewalks. I liked the smells of the trees and the colors of the trees. I liked to walk with my head up, practically hanging over my back. Then I could see the patterns the leaves formed against the blue sky.

I had my head way back and was watching the leaves when I first saw Jennifer up in the tree. She was dressed as a Pilgrim, too. I saw her feet first. She was sitting on one of the lower branches of the tree swinging her feet. That's how I happened to see her feet first. They were just about the boniest feet I had ever seen. Swinging right in front of my eyes as if I were sitting in the first row at Cinerama. They wore real Pilgrim shoes made of buckles and cracked old leather. The heel part flapped up and down because the shoes were so big that only the toe part could stay attached. Those shoes looked as if they were going to fall off any minute.

I grabbed the heel of the shoe and shoved it back onto the heel of that bony foot. Then I wiped my hands on my Pilgrim apron and looked up at Jennifer. I didn't know yet that she was Jennifer. She was not smiling, and I was embarrassed.

I said in a loud voice, which I hoped would sound stout red but which came out sounding thin blue, "You're going to lose that shoe."

The first thing Jennifer ever said to me was, "Witches never lose anything."

"But you're not a witch," I said. "You're a Pilgrim, and look, so am I."

"I won't argue with you," she said. "Witches convince; they never argue. But I'll tell you this much. Real witches are Pilgrims, and just because I don't have on a silly black costume and carry a silly broom and wear a silly black hat, doesn't mean that I'm not a witch. I'm a witch all the time and not just on Halloween."

I didn't know what to say, so I said what my mother always says when she can't answer one of my questions. I said, "You better hurry up now, or you'll be late for school."

"Witches are never late," she said.

"But witches have to go to school." I wished I had said something clever.

"I just go to school because I'm putting the teacher under a spell," she said.

"Which teacher?" I asked. "Get it? *Witch* teacher?" I laughed. I was pleased that now I had said something clever.

Jennifer neither laughed nor answered. But I was sure she'd got it. She looked at me hard and said, "Give me those three chocolate chip cookies, and I'll come down and tell you my name, and I'll walk the rest of the way to school with you."

I wasn't particularly hungry for the cookies, but I was hungry for company, so I said, "Okay," and reached out my hand holding the cookies. I wondered how she could tell that they were chocolate chips. They were in a bag.

As she began to swing down from the branches, I caught a glimpse of her underwear. I expected that it would look dusty, and it did. But that was not why it was not like any underwear I had ever seen. It was old fashioned. There were buttons and no elastic. She also had on yards and yards of petticoats. Her Pilgrim dress looked older than mine. Much older. Much, much older. Hers looked ancient. Of course, my Pilgrim costume was not new either. I had worn it the year before, but then I had been in a different grade in a different school. My cousin had worn the costume before that. I hadn't grown much during the year. My dress was only a little short, and only a little tight, and only a little scratchy where it was pinned, and it was only absolutely uncomfortable. In other words, my costume was a hand-me-down, but Jennifer's was a genuine antique.

After Jennifer touched the ground, I saw that she was taller than I. Everybody was. I was the shortest kid in my class. I was always the shortest kid in my class. She was thin. Skinny is what she really was. She came toward my hand and looked hard at the bag of cookies.

"Are you sure you didn't bite any of them?" she demanded.

"Sure I'm sure," I said. I was getting mad, but a bargain's a bargain.

"Well," she said, taking one cookie out of the bag, "My name is Jennifer. Now let's get going."

As she said "going," she grabbed the bag with the other two cookies and started to walk.

"Wait up," I yelled. "A bargain's a bargain. Don't you want to know my name?"

"I told you witches are never late, but I can't be responsible for you yet . . . Elizabeth."

She knew my name already! She walked so fast that I was almost convinced that she was a witch; she was practically flying. We got to school just as the tardy bell began to ring. Jennifer's room was a fifth grade just off the corridor near the entrance, and she slipped into her classroom while the bell was still buzzing. My room was four doors further down the hall, and I got to my room *after* the bell had stopped.

She had said that witches are never late. Being late felt as uncomfortable as my tight Pilgrim dress. No Pilgrim had ever suffered as much as I did. Walking to my seat while everyone stared at me was awful. My desk was in the back of the room; it was a long, long walk. The whole class had time to see that I was a blushing Pilgrim. I knew that I was ready to cry. The whole class didn't have to know that too, so I didn't raise my eyes until I was seated and felt sure that they wouldn't leak. When I looked up, I saw that there were six Pilgrims: three other Pilgrim girls and two Pilgrim boys. That's a lot of Pilgrims for a class of twenty. But none of them could be witches, I thought. After checking over their costumes and shoes, I decided that at least three of them had cousins who had been Pilgrims the year before.

Miss Hazen announced that she would postpone my detention until the next day because of the Halloween parade. Detention was a school rule; if you were late coming to school, you stayed after school that day. The kids called it "staying after." I didn't feel grateful for the postponement. She could have skipped my "staying after" altogether.

Our lesson that afternoon was short, and I didn't perform too well. I had to tug on my dress a lot and scratch under my Pilgrim hat a lot. I would have scratched other places where the costume itched, but they weren't polite.

At last we were all lined up in the hall. Each class was to march to the auditorium and be seated. Then one class at a time would walk across the stage before the judges. The rest of the classes would be the audience. The classes at the end of the hall marched to the auditorium first.

There were classes on both sides of the hall near my room, and the space for the marchers was narrow. Some of the children had large cardboard cartons over them and were supposed to be packages of cigarettes or sports cars. These costumes had trouble getting through. Then there was Jennifer. She was last in line. She looked neither to the right nor to the left but slightly up toward the ceiling. I kept my eye on her hoping she'd say "Hi" so that I wouldn't feel so alone standing there. She didn't. Instead, well, I almost didn't believe what I actually saw her do.

But before I tell what I saw her do, I have to tell about Cynthia. Every grown-up in the whole U.S. of A. thinks that Cynthia is perfect. She is pretty and neat and smart. I guess that makes perfect to almost any grown-up. Since she lives in the same apartment house as we do, and since my mother is a grown-up, and since my mother thinks that she is perfect, my mother had tried hard to have us become friends since we first moved to town. My mother would drop hints. HINT: Why don't you call Cynthia and ask her if she would like to show you where the library is? Then you can both eat lunch here. Or HINT: Why don't you run over and play with Cynthia while I unpack the groceries?

It didn't take me long to discover that what Cynthia was, was not perfect. The word for what Cynthia was, was *mean*.

Here's an example of mean. There was a little boy in our building who had moved in about a month before we did. His name was Johann; that's German for John. He moved from Germany and didn't speak English yet. He loved Cynthia. Because she was so pretty, I guess. He followed her around and said, "Cynsssia, Cynsssia." Cynthia always made fun of him. She would stick her tongue between her teeth and say, "Th, th, th, th, th. My name is Cyn-*th*-ia not Cyn-*sss*-ia." Johann would smile and say, "Cyn-*sss*-ia." Cynthia would stick out her tongue and say, "Th, th, th, th, th." And then she'd walk away from him. I liked Johann. I wished he would follow me around. I would have taught him English, and I would never even have minded if he called me Elizabesss. Another word for Cynthia was, was *two-faced*. Because every time some grown-up was around, she was sweet to Johann. She'd smile at him and pat his head . . . only until the grown-up left.

And another thing: Cynthia certainly didn't need me for a friend. She had a very good friend called Dolores who also lived in the apartment house. They told secrets and giggled together whenever I got into the elevator with them. So I got into the habit of leaving for school before they did. Sometimes, on weekends, they'd be in the elevator when I got on; I'd act as if they weren't there. I had to get off the elevator before they did because I lived on the second floor, and they lived on the sixth. Before I'd get off the elevator, I'd take my fists, and fast and furious, I'd push every floor button just the second before I got out. I'd step out of the elevator and watch the dial stopping at every floor on the way up. Then I'd skip home to our apartment.

For Halloween Cynthia wore everything real ballerinas wear: leotards and tights and ballet slippers and a tutu. A tutu is a little short skirt that ballerinas wear somewhere around their waists. Hers looked like a nylon net doughnut floating around her middle. Besides all the equipment I listed above, Cynthia wore rouge and eye make-up and lipstick and a tiara. She looked glamorous, but I could tell that she felt plenty chilly in that costume. Her teeth were chattering. She wouldn't put on a sweater.

As we were standing in the hall waiting for our turn to go to the auditorium, and as Jennifer's class passed, Cynthia was turned around talking to Dolores. Dolores was dressed as a Pilgrim. They were both whispering and giggling. Probably about Jennifer.

Here's what Jennifer did. As she passed Cynthia, she reached out and quicker than a blink unsnapped the tutu. I happened to be watching her closely, but even I didn't believe that she had really done it. Jennifer clop-clopped along in the line with her eyes still up toward the ceiling and passed me a note almost without my knowing. She did it so fast that I wasn't even sure she did it until I felt the note in my hand and crunched it beneath my apron to hide it. Jennifer never took her eyes off the ceiling or broke out of line for even half a step.

I wanted to make sure that everyone saw Cynthia with her tutu down, so I pointed my finger at her and said, "O-o-o-o-oh!" I said it loud. Of course, that made everyone on both sides of the aisle notice her and start to giggle.

Cynthia didn't have sense enough to be embarrassed. She loved attention so much that she didn't care if her tutu had fallen. She stepped out of it, picked it up, shook it out, floated it over her head, and anchored it back around her waist. She touched her hands to her hair, giving it little pushes the way women do who have just come out of the beauty parlor. I hoped she was itchy.

Finally, our class got to the auditorium. After I sat down, I opened the note, holding both my hands under my Pilgrim apron. I slowly slipped my hands out and glanced at the note. I was amazed at what I saw. Jennifer's note looked like this:

Meet for Trick or Treat
at
Half after six P.M. o'clock
of this evening.
By the same tree.
Bring two (2) bags.
Those were good cookies

I studied the note a long time. I thought about the note as I watched the Halloween parade; I wondered if Jennifer used a quill pen. You can guess that I didn't win any prizes for my costume. Neither did Cynthia. Neither did Jennifer (even though I thought she should have). We all marched across the stage wearing our masks and stopped for a curtsy or bow (depending on whether you were a girl or a boy) in front of the judges who were sitting at a table in the middle of the stage. Some of the girls who were disguised as boys forgot themselves and curtsied. Then we marched off. Our class was still seated when Jennifer clop-clopped across the stage in those crazy Pilgrim slippers. She didn't wear a mask at all. She wore a big brown paper bag over her head and *there were no holes cut out for her eyes*. Yet, she walked up the stairs, across the stage, stopped, and curtsied, and walked off without tripping or falling or walking out of those gigantic shoes.

Our family rushed through supper that night. But the trick or treaters started coming even before we finished. Most of the early ones were bitsy kids who had to bring their mothers to reach the door bells for them.

I didn't tell my parents about Jennifer. I mentioned to my mother that I was meeting a friend at 6:30, and we were going to trick or treat together. Mom just asked, "Someone from school?" and I just said, "Yes."

The days start getting short, and the evenings start getting cool in late October. So I had to wear my old ski jacket over my costume. I looked like a Pilgrim who had made a bad trade with the Indians. Jennifer was waiting. She was leaning against the tree. She had put on stockings. They were long, black, cotton stockings, and she wore a huge black shawl. She smelled a little bit like moth balls, but I happen to especially like that smell in autumn.

"Hi," I said.

"I'll take the bigger bag," she replied.

She didn't say "please."

I held out the bags. She took the bigger one. She didn't say "thank you." Her manners were unusual. I guessed that witches never said "please" and never said "thank you." All my life my mother had taught me a politeness vocabulary. I didn't mind. I thought that "please" and "thank you" made conversation prettier, just as bows and lace make dresses prettier. I was full of admiration for how easily Jennifer managed without bows or lace or "please" or "thank you."

She opened her bag, stuck her head way down inside, and said:

"Bag, sack, parcel post,
Fill thyself
With goodies most."

She lifted her head out of the bag and tightened her shawl. "We can go now," she said.

"Don't you mean, 'Bag, sack, parcel, *poke*'?" I asked. "Parcel *post* is the mail; *poke* is a name for a bag."

Jennifer was walking with her head up, eyes up. She shrugged her shoulders and said, "Poetic license. *Poke* doesn't rhyme."

I shrugged my shoulders and started walking with her. Jennifer disappeared behind a tree. No master spirit had taken her away. She reappeared in a minute, pulling a wagon. It was the usual kind of child's wagon, but to make the sides taller, she had stretched a piece of chicken wire all along the inner rim. Jennifer pulled the wagon, carried her bag, clutched her shawl, and clop-clopped toward the first house. I walked.

I had been trick or treating for a number of years. I began as a bitsy kid, and my mother rang the door bells for me, as other mothers were ringing them for those other bitsy kids that night. I had been a nurse, a mouse (I had worn my sleepers with the feet in), and other things. I had been a Pilgrim before, too. I mentioned that I had been a Pilgrim the year before. All I mean to say is that I'd been trick or treating for years and years and years, and I'd seen lots of trick or treaters come to our house, but I'd never, never, never seen a performance like Jennifer's.

This is the way Jennifer operated: 1. She left the wagon outside the door of the house and out of sight of her victim. 2. She rang the bell. 3. Instead of smiling and saying "trick or treat," she said nothing when the people came to the door. 4. She half fell against the door post and said, "I would like just a drink of water." 5. She breathed hard. 6. The lady or man who answered would say, "Of course," and would bring her a drink of water. 7. As she reached out to get the water, she dropped her big, empty bag. 8. The lady or man noticed how empty it was and said, "Don't you want just a little something?" 9. The lady or man poured stuff into Jennifer's bag. 10. The lady or man put a little something in my bag, too. 11. Jennifer and I left the house. 12. Jennifer dumped the treats into the wagon. 13. Jennifer clop-clopped to the next house with the bag empty again. 14. I walked.

Jennifer did this at every house. She always drank a glass of water. She always managed to drop her empty bag. I asked her how she could drink so much water. She must have had about twenty-four glasses. She didn't answer. She shrugged her shoulders and walked with her head up, eyes up. I sort of remembered something about a water test for witches. But I also sort of remembered that it was something about witches being able to float on water that was outside their bodies, not water that was inside their bodies.

I asked Jennifer why she didn't wear a mask. She answered that one disguise was enough. She told me that all year long she was a witch, disguised as a perfectly normal girl; on Halloween she became undisguised. She may be a witch, I thought, and, of course, she was a girl. But perfect never! And normal never!

I can say that Jennifer collected more treats on that Halloween than I had in all my years put together including the time I was a mouse in my sleepers with the feet in. Because I was with Jennifer each time she went into her act, I managed to collect more treats on that Halloween than I ever had before but not nearly as many as Jennifer. My bag was heavy, though.

Jennifer and I parted about a block from my apartment house. My bag was so heavy that I could hardly hold it with one hand as I pushed the button for the elevator. I put the bag on the floor while I waited. When the elevator arrived, I leaned over to pick up my bundle and heard my Pilgrim dress go *r-r-r-r-r-i-p*. I arrived at our apartment, tired and torn, but happy. Happy because I had had a successful Halloween; happy because I had not met Cynthia on the elevator; and happy because my costume had ripped. I wouldn't have to be an itchy Pilgrim another Halloween.

The Headless Cupid

Zilpha Keatley Snyder

—∗ Newbery Honor, 1972 ∗—

The four Stanley children are amazed to discover that their new stepsister, Amanda, has studied witchcraft. The children look to her to help figure out the mystery of who cut off the head of a wooden cupid on the stairway.

David often wondered about how he happened to be sitting there on the stair landing, within arm's reach of the headless cupid, at the very moment when his stepmother left Westerly House to bring Amanda home.

When Molly appeared at the foot of the stairs, David knew she was leaving because she had her shoes on and there was no paint on her hands and clothes. Molly, who at that time had been David's stepmother for about three weeks, was an artist, and around the house she dressed like an artist, very informally.

"Oh, there you are," she said to David. "I'm going now to pick up Amanda. Would you keep an eye on the kids while I'm gone? They were down by the swing a minute ago."

David said he would and Molly left, smiling back at him from the doorway. He sat a minute longer enjoying the deep silence of the big old house, empty now except for him. Even then, before anything happened, he felt there was something unusual about that spot on the landing. There was a central feeling about it, as if it were the heart of the old house. It was also a good vantage point, with a view of lots of doors and hallway, both upstairs and down.

David got up after a while and went outside and found his little brother and sisters. He pushed them in the swing until he got tired and then he took them all upstairs to the room that he shared with his brother, Blair. The kids got out some toys, and after they'd settled down, David took a book and stretched out on the window seat where he could see the driveway. He read some, but mostly he watched for Molly's car and wondered about the future—and Amanda.

Amanda, who was Molly's twelve-year-old daughter, had been staying with her own father before Dad and Molly's wedding; but now she was coming to live with her mother and the Stanley family. Suddenly to get an older sister—David was still eleven—after so many years of being the oldest, would make anybody wonder about the future. And David had a strong feeling that Amanda might give a person more to wonder about than the average stepsister.

That feeling about Amanda came partly from a few specific clues, but mostly from a premonition. Premonitions ran in David's family—on his mother's side—and the one David had about Amanda was one of the strongest he'd ever had. What it felt like was a warning, a warning to expect some drastic differences when Amanda joined the Stanley family.

Some of the specific clues came from little things Molly or David's dad had let slip, but the strongest one came from one particular facial expression. The expression had been on Amanda's face the only time David had ever met her.

David had only met Amanda once because, in all the time Dad and Molly had been going together, Amanda had managed not to be around very much. Of course Dad had seen her, but whenever something was planned for both families, Amanda usually had something terribly important come up—like a test to study for, or a sudden attack of the stomach flu. All but one time when they'd all gone to the zoo together, way back when Dad and Molly had first met.

David hadn't paid much attention to Amanda that afternoon because he had no idea then that she was going to be his stepsister, and besides he'd been busy keeping Blair away from the animals. Blair and most animals understood each other, so there really hadn't been too much danger—except from the zoo-keepers, who didn't understand about Blair at all.

David did recall saying "Hello" to Amanda when his father introduced them—and Amanda not saying anything. He could conjure up a vague picture of brownish hair and a red dress, but what he could remember best was the expression on Amanda's face. She had looked at him that same way every time he got near her all afternoon. It was the kind of look, that when people keep doing it at you, you start feeling you ought to check the bottom of your shoes—particularly when you're at the zoo. David had checked and his shoes were all right, but he hadn't forgotten that expression.

All of David's clues, and instincts, seemed to indicate that he should be prepared for almost anything, and he thought he was; he hoped he was. When Molly's little VW finally turned off the highway onto the long dusty driveway, David got up on his knees on the window seat and unlatched the window. He opened it just wide enough to see out through the crack. The glass in the old lattice windows was wavy and not much good for looking through when you were interested in details.

The car pulled up in front of the veranda steps, and for several minutes no one got out. David supposed that Molly and Amanda were in the midst of a discussion. Obviously they would have a lot to talk about. Since they'd seen each other, Dad and Molly had gotten married, gone away on a honeymoon, and come back and moved all their stuff and all the Stanley kids into the old Westerly house in the country—which happened to be the only house they could find that was big and cheap enough. And all that time Amanda had been staying with her own father in Southern California.

David was still waiting and watching when, in the room behind him, there was a loud clatter followed by a scream that sounded like a stepped-on cat. David could guess what had happened without even turning around. The last time he'd checked the kids, Janie had been building something in the corner, Esther had been cleaning the floor with her toy vacuum, and Blair had been curled up on David's bed fast asleep. Now Esther came running and climbed up beside David, and across the room Janie was standing up slowly with a clenched jaw and mean looking eyes. Esther crawled behind David and peeked out at Janie who, as usual, was getting ready to throw things.

"Stop that, Janie," David said. "Put that down. What's the matter?"

"Tesser kicked over my horse corral," Janie said, between tight teeth. Tesser was what Esther had named herself before she could pronounce Esther.

"No," Esther said from behind David. "I didn't kick over it. I *fell* over it."

Janie kept coming. "Janie," David said, "if you throw that horse, you'll break it."

"You'll break Tesser," Esther said.

David laughed, and after a moment, Janie looked at the china horse in her hand, and the red started going out of her face. David turned back to the window, thinking that Amanda was probably in the house and he'd missed seeing her, but she wasn't. Both Molly and Amanda were still sitting in the convertible. Just about then the door on Molly's side banged open, and Molly jumped out. She slammed the door behind her and walked fast across the driveway and up the steps, leaving Amanda sitting alone in the car. David couldn't see Molly's face very well, but something about the way she held her head and shoulders made him wonder if she were crying.

For another minute or two Amanda went on sitting in the car; but then her door opened very slowly and deliberately, and she got out. As soon as David got a good look at her, he leaned forward quickly, squeezing Esther into the corner of the window seat.

"Wow!" he said under his breath. Esther heard him and she shoved under his arm so that her face was under his in the crack of the window.

"Wow!" Esther said. "What's that?"

David didn't answer until Esther banged her head back against his chin and got his attention. "What's that?" she asked again.

"That?" David shook his head slowly. "That's our new sister, Tesser." And they both went on staring.

For the first second or two he'd actually thought there were a bunch of springs and wires coming out of Amanda's head, but then he realized it was only her hair. It seemed to be braided in dozens of long tight braids and some of them were looped around and fastened back to her head. The rest of her was almost covered by a huge bright colored shawl with a shaggy fringe, except for down below her knees, where something black with a crooked hem was hanging. She stood still for a minute after she got out of the car, looking after her mother; and David could see most of her face. He remembered, seeing her again, some things he'd forgotten—the very dark eyebrows, smallish nose, and the way her mouth moved now and then into what looked like an upside-down smile. But he didn't remember the spot in the middle of her forehead. It seemed to be shaped like a triangle, and when she moved, it caught and reflected the light like a tiny mirror.

She stood for a minute staring after her mother with her mouth in the upside-down smile, and then she turned back to the car. First she got out something that looked like a large dome-shaped cage covered with a beach towel, and then a couple of big suitcases. Next she opened the trunk and began lifting out boxes, lots of cardboard boxes that seemed to be filled with something very heavy. She put all the boxes and suitcases and the big cage together at the side of the driveway. She was getting two smaller cages out, when her eyes flicked upwards, and for a moment David wondered if she'd seen him in the crack of the window. But she only went on with what she was doing until everything was gathered together beside the driveway. She turned then, slowly and deliberately, and looked directly at David and Esther. There was no doubt about it. She went on looking long enough for David to be sure she really knew they were there, and then she nodded and made a motion with her hand. Both the nod and the wave meant, "Come here."

David jumped. He jumped back from the window and shut it. Esther looked up at him questioningly.

"That new sister said—like this," Esther said, making a "come here" motion with her hand.

"Yeah," David said. "I know." He opened the window again and leaned out. "Wha—who—d-did you want me?" he called.

Amanda tucked her lips in the upside-down smile and nodded, very slowly and definitely. She motioned towards the pile of boxes and bags. David got the point.

"Okay," he called. "I'll be right down."

"Right down," Esther said. She slid off the window seat, too.

David looked at her and frowned, but then he shrugged. If he stopped to argue with her, Janie would be sure to get interested, and Blair might even wake up and want to come along. And to have just one tag-along would be better than to have all three.

David nodded at Esther and said to Janie, "I'm going down to help carry boxes and things."

Janie only glanced at them and then went on rebuilding her horse corral. David had put it that way on purpose, so as not to arouse her interest, and it worked. Everyone in the whole family was sick of carrying boxes and things.

On the way down the curving staircase David held Esther's hand because if you didn't she still had to put both feet on each stair, and it took forever; but as soon as they reached the bottom he pulled his hand away. He knew from experience that some people his own age thought it was funny the way the little Stanley kids followed him around and hung on him. Of course there was a reason for it—even before she died over a year before, their mother had been sick for a long time, and a lot of the time the kids hadn't had anyone else to hang on. But you couldn't go around explaining that to everyone.

David cringed inwardly remembering the time Esther had called him Mommy, right in front of a guy he used to know named Skip Hunter. Esther hadn't meant to, of course. She was very young at the time, and Mommy was one of the few words she knew. But Skip had made a big thing out of it, and a bunch of his friends had called David "Mommy" for a long time.

Esther was still tagging along, a few feet behind, when David went down the porch steps. He could see from there that the spot on Amanda's forehead was a triangle of some kind of metallic substance, which seemed to change colors when you looked at it from different angles. Amanda stood perfectly still watching them come, with only her eyes moving from David to Esther and back again—a long blank look from unblinking eyes.

"Hi," David said; but Amanda went on staring silently for so long that he began to wonder if she was still going to refuse to speak to him, even now that they had to live in the same house. It was so weird that David had to concentrate to keep his hands and face from doing nervous twitchy things while he waited.

At last Amanda sighed and said, "You're David," making the words a part of the sigh.

Because he was so glad to have the creepy silence over with, David nodded much too enthusiastically.

"And that one?" Amanda said, pointing at Esther. "Which one is that one?"

Because of the tone of Amanda's voice, David checked Esther out to see if there was something wrong with her, like maybe her nose was running or she'd forgotten some of her clothes; but everything seemed to be in order. Esther wasn't particularly gorgeous, but she looked about average for a four-year-old girl—short and solid with straight brown hair and fat pink cheeks.

"That's—" he started, but Esther drowned him out.

"That's Tesser," she said, pointing at herself right between the eyes.

"What did she say?" Amanda asked.

"She said Tesser," David said. "That's what she calls herself."

Amanda looked a little bit more interested than David had seen her look before. "Why does she do that?" she asked.

"I don't know," David said. "Why do you call yourself Tesser?"

"Because I am Tesser," Esther said.

"It's the way she pronounces Esther," David explained.

"Oh," Amanda shrugged, "is that all. I thought maybe it was her spiritual name."

"Her what?" David asked.

"Her spiritual name."

"Oh," said David.

Esther was jerking on the back of his shirt. He told her to stop and pushed her hand away, but she started in again. Finally he said, "What is it?" and she motioned with her finger for him to lean over.

"Whisper," she said.

David sighed. Esther never screamed and threw things like Janie, but she was terribly determined. He knew he might as well let her whisper or she'd go on asking for hundreds of times. He squatted down so she could reach his ear, and she leaned over and went, "Whizawhizawhiza," in it. You never could understand a word of Esther's whispers, but this time it was pretty plain what she meant, because she kept pointing at Amanda's head.

"I think she wants to know about your hair, or that thing on your forehead," he said.

"My hair?" Amanda said, as if there weren't anything unusual about it at all.

"Why it's all—uh, all in those tight braids."

"Oh that," Amanda said. "That's part of my ceremonial costume. So's this," she added pointing to the triangle on her forehead. "This is my center of power."

"Power?" David was starting to ask, when suddenly Esther gave an excited squeal. She had lifted the corner of the beach towel and was peeking into the dome-shaped cage.

"It's a bird," she said. "David, look. It's a great big bird."

"Yeah," David said. "It sure is. It looks like a crow. Isn't it a crow?"

Amanda picked up the cage and wrapped the towel around it. "Not exactly," she said. "I'll carry the cages, and you can carry that box of books." She pointed to Esther. "And you carry that little train case."

The box of books was big and very heavy. David staggered a little going up the stairs. Behind him, Amanda was carrying the big cage in one hand and one of the little cages in the other. Behind them both, Esther came slowly, one step at a time.

When they got to the room that Molly had chosen for Amanda, David sat down on the box he'd been carrying to catch his breath. It was a small room but interesting, with dormer windows and a ceiling that slanted in all directions. Amanda looked around, blank-faced and cool-eyed as ever. David couldn't begin to guess if she liked the room or not.

He remembered then what he'd been about to ask before they started upstairs. "What did you mean—not exactly?" he said. "It's either a crow or it isn't. How comes it's 'not exactly' a crow?"

Amanda unwrapped the beach towel, and the crow sidled across its perch and pecked viciously at her fingers. "It's not exactly a crow," she said, "because it's actually a familiar spirit. I don't suppose you've ever heard the term before, but this crow is my Familiar."

The Tombs of Atuan

Ursula K. Le Guin

—:• NEWBERY HONOR, 1972 •:—

WHEN SHE WAS A CHILD, TENAR WAS STRIPPED OF HER NAME AND HER
FAMILY AND WAS SENT INTO TRAINING AS A HIGH PRIESTESS TO THE NAME-
LESS ONES, THE POWERS WHO GUARD THE CATACOMBS OF THE TOMBS OF
ATUAN.

PROLOGUE

"Come home, Tenar! Come home!"

In the deep valley, in the twilight, the apple trees were on the
eve of blossoming; here and there among the shadowed boughs
one flower had opened early, rose and white, like a faint star.
Down the orchard aisles, in the thick, new, wet grass, the little girl
ran for the joy of running; hearing the call she did not come at
once, but made a long circle before she turned her face towards
home. The mother waiting in the doorway of the hut, with the firelight behind her, watched the tiny figure running and bobbing like

a bit of thistledown blown over the darkening grass beneath the trees.

By the corner of the hut, scraping clean an earth-clotted hoe, the father said, "Why do you let your heart hang on the child? They're coming to take her away next month. For good. Might as well bury her and be done with it. What's the good of clinging to one you're bound to lose? She's no good to us. If they'd pay for her when they took her, that would be something, but they won't. They'll take her and that's an end of it."

The mother said nothing, watching the child who had stopped to look up through the trees. Over the high hills, above the orchards, the evening star shone piercing clear.

"She isn't ours, she never was since they came here and said she must be the Priestess at the Tombs. Why can't you see that?" The man's voice was harsh with complaint and bitterness. "You have four others. They'll stay here, and this one won't. So, don't set your heart on her. Let her go!"

"When the time comes," the woman said, "I will let her go." She bent to meet the child who came running on little, bare, white feet across the muddy ground, and gathered her up in her arms. As she turned to enter the hut she bent her head to kiss the child's hair, which was black; but her own hair, in the flicker of firelight from the hearth, was fair.

The man stood outside, his own feet bare and cold on the ground, the clear sky of spring darkening above him. His face in the dusk was full of grief, a dull, heavy, angry grief that he would never find the words to say. At last he shrugged, and followed his wife into the firelit room that rang with children's voices.

THE EATEN ONE

One high horn shrilled and ceased. The silence that followed was shaken only by the sound of many footsteps keeping time with a drum struck softly at a slow heart-pace. Through cracks in the roof of the Hall of the Throne, gaps between columns where a whole section of masonry and tile had collapsed, unsteady sunlight shone aslant. It was an hour before sunrise. The air was still and cold. Dead leaves of weeds that had forced up between marble pavement-tiles were outlined with frost, and crackled, catching on the long black robes of the priestesses.

They came, four by four, down the vast hall between double rows of columns. The drum beat dully. No voice spoke, no eye watched. Torches carried by black-clad girls burned reddish in the shafts of sunlight, brighter in the dusk between. Outside, on the steps of the Hall of the Throne, the men stood, guards, trumpeters, drummers; within the great doors only women had come, dark-robed and hooded, walking slowly four by four towards the empty throne.

Two came, tall women looming in their black, one of them thin and rigid, the other heavy, swaying with the planting of her feet. Between these two walked a child of about six. She wore a straight white shift. Her head and arms and legs were bare, and she was barefoot. She looked extremely small. At the foot of the steps leading up to the throne, where the others now waited in dark rows, the two tall women halted. They pushed the child forward a little.

The throne on its high platform seemed to be curtained on each side with great webs of blackness dropping from the gloom of the roof; whether these were curtains, or only denser shadows, the eye could not make certain. The throne itself was black, with a dull glimmer of precious stones or gold on the arms and back, and it was huge. A man sitting in it would have been dwarfed; it was not of human dimensions. It was empty. Nothing sat in it but shadows.

Alone, the child climbed up four of the seven steps of red-veined marble. They were so broad and high that she had to get both feet onto one step before attempting the next. On the middle step, directly in front of the throne, stood a large, rough block of wood, hollowed out on top. The child knelt on both knees and fitted her head into the hollow, turning it a little sideways. She knelt there without moving.

A figured in a belted gown of white wool stepped suddenly out of the shadows at the right of the throne and strode down the steps to the child. His face was masked with white. He held a sword of polished steel five feet long. Without word or hesitation he swung the sword, held in both hands, up over the little girl's neck. The drum stopped beating.

As the blade swung to its highest point and poised, a figure in black darted out from the left side of the throne, leapt down the stairs, and stayed the sacrificer's arms with slenderer arms. The sharp edge of the sword glittered in mid-air. So they balanced for a moment, the white figure and the black, both faceless, dancer-like above the motionless child whose white neck was bared by the parting of her black hair.

In silence each leapt aside and up the stairs again, vanishing in the darkness behind the enormous throne. A priestess came forward and poured out a bowl of some liquid on the steps beside the kneeling child. The stain looked black in the dimness of the hall.

The child got up and descended the four stairs laboriously. When she stood at the bottom, the two tall priestesses put on her a black robe and hood and mantle, and turned her around again to face the steps, the dark stain, the throne.

"O let the Nameless Ones behold the girl given to them, who is verily the one born ever nameless. Let them accept her life and the years of her life until her death, which is also theirs. Let them find her acceptable. Let her be eaten!"

Other voices, shrill and harsh as trumpets, replied: "She is eaten! She is eaten!"

The little girl stood looking from under her black cowl up at the throne. The jewels inset in the huge clawed arms and the back were glazed with dust, and on the carven back were cobwebs and whitish stains of owl droppings. The three highest steps directly before the throne, above the step on which she had knelt, had never been climbed by mortal feet. They were so thick with dust that they looked like one slant of gray soil, the planes of the red-veined marble wholly hidden by the unstirred, untrodden siftings of how many years, how many centuries.

"She is eaten! She is eaten!"

Now the drum, abrupt, began to sound again, beating a quicker pace.

Silent and shuffling, the procession formed and moved away from the throne, eastward towards the bright, distant square of the doorway. On either side, the thick double columns, like the calves of immense pale legs, went up to the dusk under the ceiling. Among the priestesses, and now in black like them, the child walked, her small bare feet treading solemnly over the frozen weeds, the icy stones. When sunlight slanting through the ruined roof flashed across her way, she did not look up.

Guards held the great doors wide. The black procession came out into the thin, cold light and wind of early morning. The sun dazzled, swimming above the eastern vastness. Westward, the mountains caught its yellow light, as did the facade of the Hall of the Throne. The other buildings, lower on the hill, still lay in purplish shadow, except for the Temple of the God-Brothers across the way on a little knoll: its roof, newly gilt, flashed the day back in glory. The black line of priestesses, four by four, wound down the Hill of the Tombs, and as they went they began softly to chant. The tune was on three notes only, and the word that was repeated over and over was a word so old it had lost its meaning, like a signpost still standing when the road is gone. Over and over they chanted the empty word. All that day of the Remaking of the Priestess was filled with the low chanting of women's voices, a dry unceasing drone.

The little girl was taken from room to room, from temple to temple. In one place salt was placed upon her tongue; in another she knelt facing west while her hair was cut short and washed with oil and scented vinegar; in another she lay face down on a slab of black marble behind an altar while shrill voices sang a lament for the dead. Neither she nor any of the priestesses ate food or drank water all that day. As the evening star set, the little girl was put to bed, naked between sheepskin rugs, in a room she had never slept in before. It was in a house that had been locked for years, unlocked only that day. The room was higher than it was long, and had no windows. There was a dead smell in it, still and stale. The silent women left her there in the dark.

She held still, lying just as they had put her. Her eyes were wide open. She lay so for a long time.

She saw light shake on the high wall. Someone came quietly along the corridor, shielding a rushlight so it showed no more light than a firefly. A husky whisper: "Ho, are you there, Tenar?"

The child did not reply.

A head poked in the doorway, a strange head, hairless as a peeled potato, and of the same yellowish color. The eyes were like potato-eyes, brown and tiny. The noise was dwarfed by great, flat slabs of cheek, and the mouth was a lipless slit. The child stared unmoving at this face. Her eyes were large, dark, and fixed.

"Ho, Tenar, my little honeycomb, there you are!" The voice was husky, high as a woman's voice but not a woman's voice. "I shouldn't be here, I belong outside the door, on the porch, that's where I go. But I had to see how my little Tenar is, after all the long day of it, eh, how's my poor little honeycomb?"

He moved towards her, noiseless and burly, and put out his hand as if to smooth back her hair.

"I am not Tenar any more," the child said, staring up at him. His hand stopped; he did not touch her.

"No," he said, after a moment, whispering. "I know. I know. Now you're the little Eaten One. But I . . ."

She said nothing.

"It was a hard day for a little one," the man said, shuffling, the tiny light flickering in his big yellow hand.

"You should not be in this House, Manan."

"No. No. I know. I shouldn't be in this House. Well, good night, little one. . . . Good night."

The child said nothing. Manan slowly turned around and went away. The glimmer died from the high cell walls. The little girl, who had no name any more but *Arha*, the Eaten One, lay on her back looking steadily at the dark.

THE WALL AROUND THE PLACE

As she grew older she lost all remembrance of her mother, without knowing she had lost it. She belonged here, at the Place of the Tombs; she had always belonged here. Only sometimes in the long evenings of July as she watched the western mountains, dry and lion-colored in the afterglow of sunset, she would think of a fire that had burned on a hearth, long ago, with the same clear yellow light. And with this came a memory of being held, which was strange, for here she was seldom even touched; and the memory of a pleasant smell, the fragrance of hair freshly washed and rinsed in sage-scented water, fair long hair, the color of sunset and firelight. That was all she had left.

She knew more than she remembered, of course, for she had been told the whole story. When she was seven or eight years old, and first beginning to wonder who indeed this person called "Arha" was, she had gone to her guardian, the Warden Manan, and said, "Tell me how I was chosen, Manan."

"Oh, you know all that, little one."

And indeed she did; the tall, dry-voiced priestess Thar had told her till she knew the words by heart, and she recited them: "Yes, I know. At the death of the One Priestess of the Tombs of Atuan, the ceremonies of burial and purification are completed within one month by the moon's calendar. After this certain of the Priestesses and Wardens of the Place of the Tombs go forth across the desert, among the towns and villages of Atuan, seeking and asking. They seek the girl-child who was born on the night of the Priestess' death. When they find such a child, they wait and they watch. The child must be sound of body and mind, and as it grows it must not suffer from rickets nor the smallpox nor any deformity, nor become blind. If it reaches the age of five years unblemished, then it is known that the body of the child is indeed the new body of the Priestess who died. And the child is made known to the Godking in Awabath, and brought here to her Temple and instructed for a year. And at the year's end she is taken to the Hall of the Throne and her name is given back to those who are her Masters, the Nameless Ones: for she is the nameless one, the Priestess Ever Reborn."

This was all word for word as Thar had told her, and she had never dared ask for a word more. The thin priestess was not cruel, but she was very cold and lived by an iron law, and Arha was in awe of her. But she was not in awe of Manan, far from it, and she would command him, "Now tell me how *I* was chosen!" And he would tell her again.

"We left here, going north and west, in the third day of the moon's waxing; for Arha-that-was had died in the third day of the last moon. And first we went to Tenacbah, which is a great city, though those who've seen both say it's no more to Awabath than a flea to a cow. But it's big enough for me, there must be ten hundred houses in Tenacbah! And we went on to Gar. But nobody in those cities had a baby girl born to them on the third day of the moon a month before; there were some had boys, but boys won't do. . . . So we went into the hill country north of Gar, to the towns and villages. That's my own land. I was born in the hills there, where the rivers run, and the land is green. Not in this desert." Manan's husky voice would get a strange sound when he said that, and his small eyes would be quite hidden in their folds; he would pause a little, and at last go on. "And so we found and spoke to all those who were parents of babies born in the last months. And some would lie to us. 'Oh yes, surely our baby girl was born on the moon's third day!' For poor folk, you know, are often glad to get rid of girl-babies. And there were others who were so poor, living in lonely huts in the valleys of the hills, that they kept no count of days and scarce knew how to tell the turn of time, so they could not say for certain how old their baby was. But we could always come at the truth, by asking long enough. But it was slow work. At last we found a girl-child, in a village of ten houses, in the orchard-vales westward of Entat. Eight months old she was, so long had we been looking. But she had been born on the night that the Priestess of the Tombs had died, and within the very hour of her death. And she was a fine baby, sitting up on her mother's knee and looking with bright eyes at all of us, crowding into the one room of the house like bats into a cave! The father was a poor man. He tended the apple trees of the rich man's orchard, and had nothing of his own but five children and a goat. Not even the house was his. So there we all crowded in, and you could tell by the way the priestesses looked at the baby and spoke among themselves that they thought they had found the Reborn One at last. And the mother could tell this too. She held the baby and never said a word. Well, so, the next day we came back. And look here! The little bright-eyed baby lying in a cot of rushes weeping and screaming, and all over its body weals and red rashes of fever, and the mother wailing louder than the baby, 'Oh! Oh! My babe hath the Witch-Fingers on her!' That's how she said it; the smallpox she meant. In my village, too, they called it the Witch-Fingers. But Kossil, she who is now the High Priestess of the Godking, she went to the cot and picked up the baby. The others had all drawn back, and I with them; I don't value my life very high, but who enters a house where smallpox is? But she had no fear, not that one. She picked up the baby and said, 'It has no fever.' And she spat on her finger and rubbed at the red marks, and they came off. They were only berry juice. The poor silly mother had thought to fool us and keep her child!" Manan laughed heartily at this; his yellow face hardly changed, but his sides heaved. "So, her husband beat her, for he was afraid of the wrath of the priestesses. And soon we came back to the desert, but each year one of the people of the Place would return to the village among the apple orchards, and see how the child got on. So five years passed, and then Thar and Kossil made the journey, with the Temple guards, and soldiers of the red helmet sent by the Godking to escort them safely. They brought the child back here, for it was indeed the Priestess of the Tombs reborn, and here it belonged. And who was the little child, eh, little one?"

"Me," said Arha, looking off into the distance as if to see something she could not see, something gone out of sight.

Once she asked, "What did the . . . the mother do, when they came to take the child away?"

But Manan didn't know; he had not gone with the priestesses on that final journey.

And she could not remember. What was the good in remembering? It was gone, all gone. She had come where she must come. In all the world she knew only one place: the Place of the Tombs of Atuan.

A Gathering of Days: A New England Girl's Journal, 1830–32

Joan W. Blos

—❧ Newbery Medal, 1980 ❧—

Through personal diary entries, fourteen-year-old Catherine Cabot Hill tells her story of a year in which she suffers much change, loss, and leave-taking.

Thursday, April 14, 1831

Mrs. Shipman considers *wasted* the day on which there is naught accomplished, and waste the worst of sins. Therefore were we three obliged–Cassie, Matty, and I together–on the *loveliest* day of Spring to each let down an outgrown frock and re-sew the hem. Cassie and I are held to the rule of twelve full stitches to the inch; Matty, younger, is spared. "Any work worth doing," recites Mrs. Shipman, "is worth doing well."

By the time I got up from the table my fingers were cramped, my neck was stiff, and indeed my whole back *ached* with the prolonged effort of bending over so close!

Saturday, April 16, 1831

Father departs on Monday for Boston. There has been very much to do in that trip's preparation. Furs must be bundled–both his own and Mr. Shipman's–for these are principal among the things he will take to trade. Also, cut and packed in blocks, is maple sugar–the work of hours–to sweeten city palates. Topping the load are brooms of straw, still retaining their golden colour and some of Summer's fragrance.

These things will allow him for cash, or in trade, to obtain the next season's supplies: such foods and herbs as we cannot grow, items for mending tools and the like, and parts for the larger contraptions required by the farm. Yard goods we cannot weave at home he will buy if the price is right, or an odd bolt strikes his fancy. Some times there is a book, or toy, or some pretty thing, or even sweets, if he's traded well.

Others in the district go to Concord to trade, it being so much nearer. But Father prefers Boston's greater choice, and claims he finds better trading for the items which he brings. It is all very much to arrange. He drives there Mr. Shipman's team–horses making better time–but as he must then also trade for them there is more to carry, coming and going back.

He will return in one week's time, all going well. Matty and I are to stay on here; Cassie's father will help with the stock as he has done before. As 'change work for this and the use of the team we're to give two days plowing when it comes time for that.

Monday, April 18, 1831

Father left this morning, long before it was light. This is to put the time to his journey, which is a long, dreary way with a wagon and no relief for the team; even the coach will take more than twenty hours for the usual run.

I packed for him some journey cake, also some pieces of hearty cheese, and the last of the Winter's apples. Tonight, if he stops at an inn to sleep, he need not spend good money to obtain his food.

Matty and I both waved him off, she standing on the gate-post to follow him with her eyes. However, the darkness obscur'd his form even before the curving road took him from our sight. A few times more we glimpsed the lantern that swung from the wagon seat. After that there were some few sounds—the creak of wheels and the horses' bells—and when there was only silence we turned back to the house.

This morning I carried over to Shipmans' a good two baskets of clothing for washing—their kettles will hold both theirs *and* ours—and Cassie and I can work together, and each have company. The day being fair, with a wind for drying, I included bed sheets & casings that otherwise might have waited.

"But what does he *do*?" I questioned Cassie, speaking of Teacher Holt. Every one knows he's stayed on the Shipmans'; tho' the term is long since ended.

The task we stood at allowed us to talk—better than on the days we sew—for we have only to tend the kettles and to keep the fires. I always find it quaint to see how shirts and trousers rise to the surface, the former waving their empty sleeves, and presently seeming to vanish beneath the sudsy, steaming waves. Soon we must wring the garments out, turning the heavier pieces between us, and drop them in a second kettle, there to continue the cleansing. But even while doing this we may talk; and talk, this day, we did!

"But what does he do?" I asked again, as the subject of my question walked across the yard.

"I hadn't noticed that he does *much*," Cassie said, sounding quite like her mother, "unless you count the time at courting—bundling with Aunt Lucy by night & mooning around by day!"

Sabbath-day, April 24, 1831

The week is wearisome and long. The house, without Father, is empty and still and Matty shadows my every step as an infant will.

Went to services both times with Shipmans; walked home with Cassie and Asa in the afternoon.

Monday, April 25, 1831

This being the day we expected Father we have not left the house. However, it is evening now and he has not come. I earnestly pray no harm has befallen the one on whom we so depend, and whom we hold so dear.

Tuesday, April 26, 1831

When again, today, we must tell ourselves that he would not come, I carried down to the cellar to keep the mince that I had made. (I used Mrs. Shipman's receipt, making only half the amount, as I had used it once before and Father pronounced it tasty.)

"'Twill be as good tomorrow," I said.

"Better," said Matty loyally, which was good of her.

Thursday, April 28, 1831

With what joy we sighted the wagon, and sped down the road to meet him before he reached the yard. I and Matty had much to say, whereat he called us "Magpies, both!" and claimed to have the best news of all would we but let him tell it.

He is going to marry, he said! She is widowed, a Mistress Ann Higham, and has a son my age!

> *Letter to me from Mistress Higham*
> (It was tucked in a bonnet for me which she had selected.)
>
> My very dear Catherine,
> May I call you so? I feel that I care for you very much, can only love you more.
> The bonnet is blue, because of your eyes, of which your father told me.
> I know I shall have much to learn; and pray you will be my help & friend, as I hope to be yours,
> Ann Higham

Saturday, April 30, 1831

On Thursday evening the Shipmans were here; yesterday Uncle Jack. Mrs. Shipman is overjoyed that she'll soon have a neighbour woman, while Uncle Jack too roughly jokes he'll be the next to fall.

Father keeps telling the story over—"Went in to a shop to buy me some goods and found, instead, a wife!" Then he explains that the boy is named Daniel, and never had a father. The young husband died a scant two weeks before the son was born. In these difficult circumstances, and having herself and the babe to feed, Mistress Higham had *taken up* her brother's offer to board with him and help out in his shop. Her labour being exchanged for the lodging she hadn't felt beholden to him; and there she had stayed these twelve, thirteen, years; and there she had met my father.

Monday, May 2, 1831

A letter which Father received today confirms that they shall marry in Boston at the end of the month.

Is not late May an odd time for a wedding, with so much here that has to be done, and with Spring plowing and planting?

Joy and sorrow, says our father, each makes its own season.

Friday, May 6, 1831

A Jew, a peddlar, came by today, the first Jew I have seen. His hair was long and his beard was scant, but it hung uncut. We did not ask him in to the house, but offered food and cyder to him, of which he took only the latter.

I bought of him some needles and buttons, also sewing silk. He had scissors for sale at 12¢ each and some for twice that amount. When I inquired the difference between, such amusement came in to his eyes his whole face was transformed!

"Well now, I'll tell you," he said with a smile, "and my compliments, miss!" Then he explained that when first on the road he sold his wares as cheap as he might so to increase his trade. But customers told of his prices believed he carried tawdry stuff. To put the principle to the test he made two packets of the self-same scissors, calling some "fine" and the others "good buys," and found that people preferred the more costly, supposing them to be better. Since then his goods are more dearly priced. "Except," he concluded merrily, "for someone with sharp eyes, like yourself!" And leaving me to ponder this statement he climbed up to his seat.

Such a curious fellow, and likeable in his candor. I hope when he comes by again he'll not neglect to call.

Saturday, May 7, 1831

I told Asa about the Jew. He was sorry he had not seen him.

Monday, May 9, 1831

Again a letter for Father from *her*! And Father makes no secret of it; he is as eager as a boy, and specially goes to the bridge on Mondays so as to be there when the mail's handed down from the Boston coach.

Her letters are neatly sealed and folded, and with a well-schooled hand. Beside them my own look poor and untidy, hard tho' I may try.

Cassie, known to be delicate, is this week indisposed.

Tuesday, May 10, 1831

A new pine dresser was installed today, a large and handsome piece.

Using salt and vinegar, we rubbed the pewterware till it shone, then set it out on the dresser. If we'll not use it until she comes, it will retain its lustre, and such is my intent.

Father goes in two weeks' time. He is very hard pressed these days to put all in order. It came to me 'tis the very last time that this, our house, will be ours alone, not also hers, and Daniel's.

Friday, May 13, 1831

A cold rain, with grey skies, and chilly underfoot. Not much pleasure in bare feet today, especially as they are unaccustomed, after the leathern housing of Winter, to go about unprotected.

Matty hops from stone to stone, rubs one foot 'gainst the other one's leg, looking very like a cricket–and very streaked besides!

"I *have* to do it," she explains, sensing my disapproval. "That's the way I get them warm, and–honest!–I'll wash myself!"

Father, at least, is pleased with the rain, well-timed before Spring planting.

Saturday, May 14, 1831

Father has had a jacket made lest he appear too rude a sort in city company.

"Will not your old one do," I asked, "the one you wore at Closing Day, and still put on for church?"

"Now, miss," he said, "we'll have none of your sulks, and none of your savings either. I tell you we are *fortunate* that Mistress Higham has accepted to make her home with us."

So the new jacket–sewn for a fee!–by a seamstress-woman in town. It is grey, as a sheep's wool is. The colour becomes him nicely. The stuff should wear very well, I think, it being closely woven.

Tuesday, May 17, 1831

"Shall I have need of this or that? Please ask Catherine if . . . ?" Yesterday's letter abounded with questions which Father read aloud. He seems not to think it odd that she should be so unknowing and so unashamed. "'Tis good," he approves, "that she thinks to ask. How many others would? Come then, Catherine, what shall I say? Or do you prefer to prepare a reply that I may carry with me, it being of women's work?"

Even Cassie who is my friend is wont to take her side! "After all,

Catherine," she enjoins. "It must be ever so *diff'rent* for her, living in Boston till now."

Wednesday, May 18, 1831

Father departed this morning. Again he drove the Shipmans' team, both to hasten the journey and better present himself. The wagon itself we washed with care and have recovered the seat. The case in which Father packed his clothes bulged with the new-made woolen jacket, a fine linen shirt (of Mr. Shipman's), and other items, his own and borrowed, that he will wear for the wedding itself or in the course of his stay.

Also in the back of the wagon were some brooms to be traded. "Might as well" and "No reason not!" They fetched an excellent price last month; he hopes they will do so again. Also he took more maple sugar, and for the same reason. (We do not generally trade two times. But Father's determined to make a fair impression on Mistress Higham's family, and will not appear before them without his pockets lined.)

He gave us each a kiss on parting. "Look after your sister," were his words to me; then quickly he mounted the wagon seat and adjusted the reins. I did my best to return his smile, and waved till he was gone.

Sunday, May 22, 1831

On this day, in Boston, they married. I will not call her Mother.

Thursday, May 26, 1831

She is less tall than I expected–smaller, even, than Mrs. Shipman; and plainer than Aunt Lucy.

Daniel, too, is plain. He, however, is rather tall, with a sprinkling of freckles, and none too large a jaw. Just below the crown of his head his hair sticks out in a little tuft. D. brushes it often, in nervous gesture, but this avails him not.

"Yes, sir," "No, sir," and "Thank you, sir" were all he said today.

'Tis quite a different brother we've got than I expected, knowing the Shipman boys.

Later

Soon, for the first time, when we go up to sleep, D. will go up with us. He will use the farther quarter, towards the Western side. Mr. Shipman and David this week helped carry up a new straw mattress and a roped bed frame. There is space alongside for a box of possessions such as D. may have thought to bring. Father, now that he is returned, says he'll gladly drive some pegs for Daniel to hang his clothes upon–as many as he'll need.

Matty stares and stares. Meeting up with me she whispered, "Did you see, Cath, did you see? He's got freckles *inside* his ears!"

Friday, May 27, 1831

Tho' I know full well they gawked at the windows when Father's wagon came up the road, the Shipmans waited until today before they made a call.

"We thought you might be tired a bit, from the exhaustion of the journey–and here, you see, we've brought you some pudding–'tis simple fare, but we're farmers here, but my sister, who is from Salem, enjoys it when she's here."

Alas for Mrs. Shipman! I know she'd awaited with eagerness for her new neighbour's arrival. Yet she, on this occasion of meeting, was awkward and out of grace. Perhaps she feared the Boston woman would scorn her country ways.

But the Boston woman had worries of her own. "So very kind of you," she smiled. "The pudding will be delicious, I'm sure! Won't you please sit down? Here, let me draw up a chair for you; unless, of course, I didn't mean–well, perhaps, it *ought* to stay by the window's light?"

Our Father stood there, quite dispossess'd till, arriving later than the others, Aunt Lucy saved the day!

"I hear you've come from Boston," she said–as if they'd talked of anything else for the past two weeks! "Tell me," she said, "is it true about . . ." And all at once there were bursts of chatter; the ladies, at least, at ease.

Sabbath-day, May 29, 1831

All eyes turned when we entered the church. Father looked careful and very proud–again wore his new grey jacket. She seemed shy–as well she might–and kept her eyes cast down.

Daniel walked between me and Matty, looking straight ahead. People were curious, mostly kind. But when my ears caught someone's whisper–"She's hardly got the first one's looks"–I quickly hoped it escaped her hearing, although I think it true.

The day being mild we walked home slowly; Father talked gently all the while, as if to ease the awkwardness at being so much on view.

Monday, May 30, 1831

Around us all is fresh new green; new grass, small flowers, new leaf. On such a day it is hard to recall the recent bogginess under foot, the heavy mud on the roads.

This morning we carried down armloads of bedding, Matty and I at her direction, to air in the fresh Spring sun. Some, not having been used of late, gave off a musty smell.

Once she paused, looking out at the hills, and spoke so softly as to make me think I was not meant to hear: "Let me remember this thankful moment later, when I've doubts." Certainly it was a curious thing for a new wife to say. Another time, as she folded a quilt: "Such fine work here; and made for use! May I be proven worthy to carry on the task."

Tuesday, May 31, 1831

Talk started up about the Jew–who had seen him and who had not and from whence he came. Uncle Jack, who chanced to be here, said it put him in mind of a story which he then put to Father.

"A man there was who held that Italian was his favourite tongue. In argument with a Bible scholar, the latter preferring the Hebrew Language, the former was heard to remark:

"'You can't deny that when God Almighty thrust poor Adam out of Eden he spake Hebrew to him.'

"'That may be,' the scholar replied, 'But I take it as *certainty* that if God spake *Hebrew* when Adam was ejected, Eve was speaking *Italian* when Adam was seduced.'"

Father slapped his knee at this and, as if to recall his pleasure, repeated the final line.

Pleased by his story's great success Uncle Jack chuckled, winked, and said: "And they waste pupils' good time these days on the study of Greek?"

"Please," she said, compressing her lips, "there are children here."

She said no more, nor had to. Uncle Jack left soon thereafter, saying that he had "much to do," and firmly refusing our Father's entreaties to reconsider and stay. Afterwards Father fussed about, finally bursting forth to say, "You *know* he meant no offense!"

Wednesday, June 1, 1831

How different are the dresses she's brought from those of Cassie's mother. Yet freely she pegs an apron around them, puts a shawl atop them when chilled, and goes about as if unconcerned at her odd appearance. Open V's at throat and back, and well-shaped bodices tightly tucked, were never meant for farm work, or the country life.

Friday, June 3, 1831

Now are we busy from dawn to dusk with things she finds in need of doing, and all with our assistance! I think I have not seen Cassie to speak since she, & D., arrived.

The last of the bedding has been brought down, including the quilts my own mother brought when she came as a bride. I worry lest she should inquire why there are only eleven of these instead of the usual dozen. How little we knew when we put it out what was to befall.

Within the house we scrub and sweep. You would not think that before she came *I* had cleaned it well! This, it seems, is Spring Cleaning–and must be done from top to bottom whether 'tis needed or no. Today she enlisted Daniel's help to carry out (and in again) all the furnishings! Some of the pieces are assigned new places; the old planked table's drawn near the hearth, the fashion, she says, in Boston. She intends to hang it with a cloth, and set a lamp in the middle. The dresser's been moved to a farther wall– handier to the work of the kitchen in her estimation. Still does the new chair retain its place, and the settle's still by the fire.

Last night I sat there next to her while Father read from the Bible as he so likes to do. Daniel and Matty had been out of doors but came inside with darkness. Then joining together, five voices as one, we easily followed Father in prayer, and so retired to bed.

Dicey's Song

Cynthia Voigt

—❖ Newbery Medal, 1983 ❖—

Keeping her family together after her mother is institutionalized is what thirteen-year-old Dicey Tillerman does best. But now that all four Tillerman children have found a new home with their grandmother, Dicey has to learn the hard lesson of letting go.

What a day, Dicey thought. What a summer, for that matter, but especially, What a day. She stood alone in the big old barn, in a patch of moonlight; stood looking at the sailboat resting on its sawhorse cradle, a darker patch among shadows. Behind her, the wind blew off the water, bringing the faint smell of salt and the rich, moist smell of the marshes.

You never knew where a road would end, Dicey thought, the breeze curling around her ears, you just knew that roads ended. Not like water, which always kept moving. Not like the stars, tossed out across the sky—the stars had made that light millions of years ago and already they were burning with new light. And the moon too, the moon would swell and dwindle, go dark and swell again. But the Tillermans traveled on a road, and roads ended. Dicey's road, and James's, Maybeth's, Sammy's, had ended here. The Tillermans' road had rolled up against Gram's house, and they had tumbled off it into Gram's—Dicey grinned. Not exactly into Gram's arms, maybe not into her lap. Certainly into her life.

So. So they were going to live here, on the rundown farm, with Gram—Dicey's heart danced again, inside her, to say it to herself like that. Home. *Home with their momma's momma, who was also a Tillerman. Home: a home with plenty of room for the four children in the shabby farmhouse, room inside, room outside, and the kind of room within Gram too—Dicey had seen Gram and how she listened when Maybeth sang, how she talked with James, how her eyes smiled at the things Sammy said and did—the kind of room that was what they really needed. One of the lessons the long summer had taught Dicey was how to figure out what they really needed.*

Dicey studied her sneakers, gray with old grime, the places where her toes had worn through pockets of darkness. When she wiggled her toes in the moonlight's shadows, she couldn't see anything moving. Home for Dicey, too, with the Bay—the Chesapeake Bay, quiet with little waves and long tides—the Bay just out of sight, with this grandmother whose character had sharp corners and unexpected turns, with the sailboat waiting here in the barn.

She stepped into the darkness and placed both her hands flat against the rough hull of the boat. Imagining how it would feel when the little boat rode on the water, how it would respond to the wind in its sails, to the waves sliding by, to her hand on the tiller. She leaned her forehead against the wood, feeling the solid curve of the hull against her skin. Unexpectedly, she found herself yawning, a huge, hollow yawn that stretched her diaphragm up against her heart and cracked the hinges of her jaw.

Dicey smiled to herself. Here it was, probably the most exciting day of her life, certainly one of the best, and all she felt was tired. As if all the walking and worrying, all the hunger and hope of the long summer, all hit her at once. Her bones sagged and her brain couldn't grab onto any ideas. The muscles that held her bones in working order ached, but not a hurting ache, kind of a contented throb.

Dicey yawned again. She guessed she'd better get to bed, but she guessed she knew why she didn't want to: this happiness blew through her like wind, buoyed her up like water, and she wanted to float along on it. But the summer had worn her out, like it had worn out her sneakers; and tomorrow she'd have to start school, but on the weekend she'd get the boat into the water and learn how to sail it; the long summer stretched behind them, they'd made it through, made it home.

On the days when Sammy rode along behind James on the paper route, Dicey picked up the mail on her way home. It was early in October when Gram got an answer to her letter to the hospital in Boston where Momma was. Dicey found the letter among a pile of advertising circulars in the mailbox. She stuffed all the mail into her science notebook.

Dicey would have liked to just leave the circulars or to have returned them to the senders, but Gram said they'd use them to start fires when the weather got cold. Dicey doubted that it ever got cold here in southern Maryland. By October on the Cape, back home, the air was crisp and the leaves were turning colors, and the sand had lost all of its summer warmth. Here, all that happened so far was the water in the Bay turned clear and you could see to the shallow sandy bottom. And the leaves on the paper mulberry were turning a yellowy green. The nights were chilly, but the days were warm enough for the children's shorts to be comfortable. But Gram promised Dicey there would be cold weather coming.

Gram already had Sammy at work chopping up kindling with a small ax. She had forewarned Dicey that they were going to need to take the big, two-handled saw to a couple of fallen trees one of these weekends. Dicey had groaned at this, knowing that the time would have to be taken from the slow work on the boat. At the rate she was going, it would never be ready for the water next spring. But she had groaned silently.

Dicey showed the Boston letter to Gram, who was making bread at the kitchen table. Gram looked at it out of the side of her eyes, grunted and continued kneading. Dicey ate an apple and waited. When they sat down together, Gram looked at Dicey before she opened the envelope. "I hope you're not expecting good news," she said.

"I'm not expecting anything," Dicey answered impatiently. "I just want to know what it says."

"I'm not expecting good news," Gram said. She opened the envelope carefully with steady fingers.

It was a long letter, typed, three pages. Gram read it once quickly, then again slowly. She didn't show Dicey the pages she was finished with. Dicey bit her lip with impatience and tried not to fidget. When Gram finished the second reading, she folded the papers back into the envelope and then folded her fingers tightly together.

Dicey waited. Gram's mouth was straight and her eyes stared vacantly at the envelope.

Dicey waited.

"I need a cup of tea," Gram announced. She went to the stove to heat water. When her back was to Dicey, she said, "No change."

"None at all?" Dicey asked. She kept her voice level, hiding her own disappointment. She spoke as matter-of-factly as Gram did.

"So we'll go ahead with the adoption," Gram said. Dicey stared at her, at the strong back under the loose clothing, at her tanned legs and bare feet. "We can get to work on those forms, now we know."

"What did they say?" Dicey asked.

"I told you once, girl, no change. Are you listening?"

But the letter was three pages long. It didn't take three pages to write *no change*. "What if we went to see her?" Dicey asked.

"Do you know how much that would cost?"

Whatever it cost it would be too much.

Gram dunked the teabag in her cup, then set it aside to be used again. She turned and looked at Dicey. "Life is a hard business," she remarked.

"Was it bad news?" Dicey asked, even though she knew she shouldn't.

"Don't you listen?" Gram demanded. There was anger in her voice and in her dark hazel eyes.

"It doesn't take three pages to say *no change*," Dicey answered, her own anger rising. But *she* was angry because she was worried and frightened.

Gram snorted. "For doctors it does," she said. "I don't want you making the mistake of thinking life isn't going to be hard," she said again.

"I know that," Dicey said.

"I guess I do. I'm a natural fool," Gram said, "I keep trying to count on things. And Sammy's too young for that long bike ride. Maybe," Gram said.

Dicey knew what the woman was thinking, how the connections were made behind her eyes. But she was glad nobody was there to hear how Gram's mind jumped around.

"I'm going to the barn, if that's all right," Dicey said. She waited for her grandmother to answer. If Gram wanted Dicey to stay, for company, Dicey would like that. But Gram just said, "Suit yourself." Dicey shrugged and went out to get a little work done on the boat, and she did not let herself wonder what it was Gram had been counting on. Because Gram said the letter said no change.

October went on. The children were settling in, just as fall was settling in, over the farm and the water, into shades of brown: the harrowed soil, the dried summer grasses, the broken stalks of corn, and the long golden bars of sunlight from a sun setting closer to seven now than eight. Gram had filed all of her forms, with the lawyer's help. Now they awaited action on the fat folders filled with copies of the children's birth certificates and school records, with government papers in triplicate, saying everything that could be written down in numbers about Gram and the farm, about Momma and the kids.

Sammy mostly left Dicey alone with the boat, and when he did come bother her (she had one side more than half done by then) seemed interested only in asking questions, about how the Indians scalped people and whether there were ghosts, about the ragged bottom of the big barn doors. "Do you think someone did that on purpose?" he asked, fingering the broken-off boards. "Dicey? If you hit at it with a bat, or a sledge hammer."

"How's school?" Dicey asked.

"Fine I guess," Sammy told her, not interested in the subject. Well, at least he wasn't coming home with black eyes and bruises and ripped clothes, the way he had from school in Provincetown and from summer camp in Bridgeport. As long as Sammy wasn't fighting, Dicey wasn't going to worry about him.

James worked hard, reading and taking notes for his report. He'd decided on a topic, "Why the Pilgrims came to America." "It's interesting," he said, but he didn't want to talk about it. "It's nice to have something to do again," he told them.

Maybeth came home from school one day with an invitation to a birthday party. "You can ride your bike and I'll ride mine to pick you up," Dicey said, because it would be getting dark when the party was over. "What'll you do about a present?" Dicey didn't know what a guest at a birthday party was supposed to do.

"I thought I'd make something," Maybeth told her. "With pine cones. Gram will help. Will you help, Gram?"

"Of course, I will. But you can't wear your shorts and T-shirt."

All the children's clothes had to be practical. They had shorts and shirts, that was all. "That doesn't matter," Maybeth said.

"Maybe it really doesn't," James said to his grandmother. "Do you know who else is invited, Maybeth? Is it the whole class?"

"Just some of us," she told him. "The cake's going to have pink frosting."

Maybeth was making friends, and Sammy seemed not to be getting into trouble, and James was working hard. Dicey herself had what might be called a friend in Mina. They'd gotten A's on their rock classification project, and Mina always greeted Dicey at school, whenever she saw her, "Hey, Dicey, how you doing." Dicey always answered, "Pretty good and you," the way you were supposed to. Then she beat a fast path to her desk, or the next class. She didn't want anybody to think she was trying to have friends.

She had seen the guitar-playing boy a couple of times. The first time, she had walked right up and asked him the words for that song about the coat of many colors. He remembered her. After a while, she saw him every day it wasn't raining. He was sitting in the same place, playing his guitar when she rushed out to get on her bike and go to work. He told her his name, Jeff, and asked her hers. "Dicey Tillerman," she said, and waited for what he would say next.

"You related to that old lady with the farm?" he asked. Dicey nodded, her chin high. "What are you, a grandchild?" Dicey nodded again. "Listen, you can sing the melody of that song?" he asked her. "I want to try a harmony." Dicey could and did, listening to his voice as he made a harmony line with what she was singing, sometimes blending, sometimes moving in contrast. She thought he was fancying it up too much, but she didn't say so. And she liked singing that song, even though she didn't understand the story of it. "You sing pretty well," Jeff remarked.

"Not particularly," Dicey told him. "Just better than you. My sister is the one who can really sing. You should hear her sing this song."

"I'd like to," he said, his face friendly. What did he expect her to do, invite him to her house or something? There was something he expected, or wanted, Dicey could see that.

"I gotta go now," she said.

"Why?" he asked. "I've got another song you might like."

"I gotta go," Dicey insisted and turned away to get her bike out of the rack and ride away.

Millie never minded if Dicey was a few minutes late. She didn't seem to notice. The business continued to improve, Dicey thought; Millie never said anything, as if she had forgotten the terms of their deal. The third week came and went without a word from Millie. And the fourth week. The only thing Millie said about business to Dicey happened when Dicey came in to find her at the checkout counter studying a long printout. Behind her, all over one of the aisles, boxes of dried cereal were spread around. Millie was reading down the sheet, her lips moving silently, her fingers moving along under the words.

"Want me to put those up on display?" Dicey offered.

"I dunno where they came from," Millie said. "I dunno where they'll fit."

"You didn't order them?"

Millie shook her head. Dicey looked around for what to do. The windows could wait another day or two, or they could be washed right away. The floor–needed a damp mopping she decided. The windows could wait.

"Oh no," Millie spoke behind her. "Look what I did. Sometimes I'm so *stupid.* Just look at that."

Dicey looked over her shoulder. The page was the distributor's order sheet. Millie had filled it out in pencil, changing her mind many times, as Dicey could tell by the erasures and crossings out. "I meant to order corn chips and I ordered corn flakes. I'll never sell all these boxes. What'll I do?"

"Can't you send them back?"

"But the corn chips are for people who want them. I always have them."

"Or have a special sale on corn flakes," Dicey suggested. How could Millie have mistaken those two words?

"I hate the ordering, I always make mistakes, and I have to check it all the time. Herbie–he tried to teach me how to do it, but he gave up."

The sheet looked pretty simple to Dicey. You just found the items you wanted and put the number you wanted in a little box beside the name and then figured out how much it cost and copied that down. "How can you make mistakes on this?" she asked.

"Because I never learned how to read, not properly. I can't even read a newspaper. You didn't know that, did you. You didn't know what a stupid old woman you were working for."

"But you went to school," Dicey told her. "You said you went to school with Gram."

Millie laughed, but it wasn't a happy sound. "They kept me back some, when I was littler. Then, I got so big it was embarrassing to them, and I always behaved myself. So they'd just pass me on. I never graduated, didn't Ab tell you? No, she's no gossip. It doesn't matter and it didn't then, because I was going to get married. Herbie didn't care. He liked me the way I was. You wouldn't understand, you're one of the smart kids."

"You can't read?" Dicey was amazed.

"Of course, I can read," Millie said patiently. "I just take so long at it, and the words all look alike. I don't know, maybe now with all the machines they have for teaching, maybe now I could have learned. But it's too late for me."

Dicey didn't know what to say. "If you told me what you wanted I could fill out the order sheets," she finally offered.

Millie's face showed hope. "Do you think so? You're awfully young."

"Sure," Dicey answered. "I don't have any idea of what you should stock in, but I can read names and numbers."

"That would be a load off my mind," Millie said. "It's gotten so, since Herbie died, the distributor won't let me return things any more if I make a mistake. And then," she confided, "I get so nervous about making a mistake I go over it again and again, and it takes so long, and I can't think properly about it. Sometimes I cross out what I wanted to order and order the wrong things. As if I *wanted* to do it wrong."

Dicey nodded and kept her face expressionless. "Then you do want me to stay on," she said.

"Stay on? Here? Of course," Millie said, "what made you think I didn't? I can't handle all this business alone."

"I was just making sure," Dicey said quickly.

Dicey rode home to Gram's house these October days through sunlight turning golden and red, stopped by the mailbox (wondering each time why Gram had said nothing to the little kids about that letter from the doctor in Boston) and put in a quick half-hour's work on the boat. She had accepted the slowness with which she was going to make progress. She kept herself from being impatient, just as she kept herself private at school.

After supper these days, and before she dashed through her own homework, she read with Maybeth for a half hour or so, the two of them at the kitchen table. Maybeth had lists of words that she was supposed to memorize, vocabulary sheets. In the reading book, these words appeared in the stories. Mrs. Jackson had told Maybeth that if she stumbled on a word in a story, then she should go back and memorize the list again. So most of the time poor Maybeth was guessing her way through a list of twenty words, and Dicey would stop her when she made a mistake and Maybeth would go back to the top of the list and start again. Maybeth didn't seem discouraged, but Dicey sure was.

She thought about Maybeth and Millie; and she didn't want Maybeth to be like Millie when she grew up. It wasn't that Dicey didn't like Millie, because she did. It was all right, working for Millie. Dicey was learning a lot about how to run a grocery store, and she hoped that sometime Millie might show her how to butcher the sides of meat. But it wasn't interesting, not like other people she had worked for, when she had conversations with them. She felt pretty sorry for Millie, so big and slow-witted. She wanted something better than Millie's life for Maybeth.

Maybeth plugged along, reading, math, social studies. She never practiced her piano until everything else was done.

At the piano, at least, Maybeth moved fast. The scales had given way to the rhythmic exercises and to real pieces, with chords. James, studying the music in one of the books Mr. Lingerle loaned Maybeth, said he couldn't figure out how she could read the notes off onto the piano keys. Maybeth said it wasn't hard. James said he thought it looked harder than reading words. Maybeth shook her head, no, and went back to the piece she was playing.

Gram took an old blouse of hers, with tiny flowers printed on it, and cut it down to make a dress for Maybeth to wear to the birthday party. It took her a week, every night, to finish it. It wasn't a great dress, but Maybeth looked pretty in it. She was so excited, she whirled around the living room, letting the skirt swirl out.

James showed Dicey his report on the pilgrims. Dicey only read it because he wanted her to so badly, but once she'd started she found herself really interested. James had written about *all* the reasons why the Mayflower people wanted to come to America. He had found out who they all were and where they'd come from, and what had happened to them once they got to Plymouth. Dicey was surprised at what he was saying. Only some of the people came over for religious reasons, and even those (as James pointed out) hadn't come because of a belief in religious freedom. They came over to practice their own religion, which was a very different thing from what Dicey had always heard. Some of the people came because they weren't welcome in the society of England, because they were sort of rotten apples there. Some came because they had to, like wives, children, and indentured servants. Some came because they wanted to live and work in a land that civilization hadn't already polished and divided, because they loved wildness, because they wanted to match themselves up against the wilderness and see how they did. Dicey could understand that feeling. Some of the settlers were looking for easy money, gold or furs, to get rich quick.

"It's really good," she said to James when she finished reading. He was standing anxiously behind her.

"You think so?"

"It's interesting," Dicey said. "I bet it's the best report anybody does—I bet it's miles better than any other report in your class. I'll tell you," she said, overwhelmed into honesty by the impression it made on her, "I don't think I could write one this good."

James tried not to look as pleased as he felt. "You think Gram would like to read it?" he asked.

At about that time, Mr. Chappelle assigned Dicey's class a paper. He wanted them to write a character sketch, he said, about a real character they had met, someone they knew. He wanted them to show the conflict in a real person's life. As soon as he said that, the complaints and questions began. Dicey stopped paying attention. She knew who she'd like to write about, she knew a whole lot of people. Momma, for one; but she couldn't, because that wasn't any of his business. Will Hawkins was another. She'd like writing about him. Not about the way he'd been a good friend to the children, taken them along with his circus and driven them down to Crisfield; and not even about what it was like to live with a circus, although that would be interesting. Dicey would write about the way Will was so honest with his friends, yet tricked the people who came to his shows. Because the circus was like that, full of tricks that you didn't know about until, like the four children, you had lived in it. Probably the people who came to see the shows didn't care, but it wasn't what the people wanted that interested Dicey. She wanted to write about those two opposite sides of Will. Maybe, if she wrote about him, she could figure out how he fit those two sides together in his life; maybe he did it by keeping them entirely separate, his friends and his work. She thought about him, traveling now around the country with his circus. He'd promised to come to see them when the circus came back to the area, and she believed he would.

And there was Cousin Eunice, back in Bridgeport. In Dicey's opinion, Cousin Eunice was a boring person, but she had conflicts too. She too had taken the children in. But she had only done it because she wanted people to think she'd done the right thing. What she really wanted to do was live the life she'd planned for herself before the Tillermans turned up. She didn't want the children, they were nothing but trouble to her, trouble and expense; but she'd made herself change all her plans.

Dicey might just write something as good as James, she thought, the ideas tumbling around in her head. Then she corrected herself: almost as good as James. James was just too smart for her to keep up with.

Maybe she *could* write about Momma. If she called her Mrs. Liza, then Mr. Chappelle wouldn't ever guess who she really was. If she just didn't say certain things.

After class, Mina waited for Dicey by the door. "This essay might be fun," Mina said. "I've got an idea."

Dicey didn't know why Mina wanted to talk to her. They hurried on through the crowded halls to home ec.

"I'd like to talk to you about it," Mina said.

"Sure," Dicey said. She usually liked Mina's ideas.

"How about after school?"

"Can't," Dicey said. Mina waited for her to say more, but Dicey didn't. She wasn't sure why she didn't, except that the more anybody knew about her . . . they had a kind of hold on her. She wasn't sure, anyway, how Mina would feel about Dicey having a job, if Mina would feel sorry for her.

"You want to come by my house?" Mina asked.

"Can't," Dicey said.

Mina looked at her and Dicey looked right back. Contradictory expressions were on Mina's face, a little confusion and some anger and some laughter. Mina chose to laugh. "You sure are a hard person to be friends with, Dicey Tillerman."

Was that what Mina was doing? Dicey was so surprised, because Mina had lots of friends already, she didn't even answer. They entered the horrible home ec class, where they were supposed to be making work aprons, using everything they had learned about cutting and sewing, hems and buttons. Dicey had figured out a way to avoid most of the button troubles, a pretty clever way, she thought. The rules were you had to have two buttons on it and a hem and a tie around the neck. Dicey was following the rules, but in her own way.

It had gotten so she could almost count on seeing Jeff after school, over by the bike racks. He'd call out to her, "Hey, Dicey."

She would saunter over. "You ever hear this one?" he'd ask, and play her a song. Some of them, a lot of them, she already knew. Once, because it was in her mind for some reason, she asked him to play one of Momma's favorites, "The water is wide, I cannot go o'er." He didn't know it, said he'd never heard it, but a couple of days later he had it ready for her.

Usually, Dicey would stay and sing with him, because she liked singing. A couple of times, he asked her about her sister who could sing so well, but Dicey never told him much. She thought, though, Maybeth would like Jeff. He was in tenth grade, he said, and he reminded Dicey that she was in eighth. "I know that," Dicey answered. "So do I," he said, peering up at her from where he sat bent over his guitar. The conversation was stupid, but she smiled. He smiled back, but she had to get to work so she didn't bother finding out whether he thought it was stupid too.

One day, when Dicey came up to the back porch under a gray sky, her hands and shorts flecked with some of the paint she had scraped, she heard the piano playing a rolling, rippling melody, one that you couldn't ever sing along with. There were no words that could keep up with the notes that swept from bass up through tenor to soprano. The piano was the only voice that could manage to sing that song. She stopped and listened, dumbfounded. How had Maybeth gotten so very good all at once?

She stepped into the kitchen and saw Maybeth sitting down at the table with Gram. Their heads were bent down over a reading book. Beside them was one of the word lists Mrs. Jackson never ran out of, Maybeth read aloud, word by stumbling word. You could hear her guessing. Dicey followed the music down the hall.

A man sat at the piano. He was so fat that his fanny hung down over the back of the bench. He was fat like a cartoon fat person. For a minute, Dicey saw nothing but fatness, then looked at the details. The back of his head had a bald spot, a pink circle with a few stray hairs carefully combed over it, as if he were trying to hide it. Like trying to hide a basketball under three shoelaces, Dicey thought. His eyes and nose and mouth were all buried in the flesh of his face, and his double chins hung down. His hands, despite looking thick and clumsy at the ends of huge arms, danced over the piano keys. He was concentrating so hard—adjusting his position on the bench as the chords took him up and down the keyboard, staring down at the keys under his fingers–that sweat ran down by his ear and his shirt was stained under the armpits. His mouth was open as if he was panting. And the music poured out of the piano like a stream pouring down the side of a mountain, or like the wind pouring over the bending branches of trees.

Dicey stood, listening.

After a while, the music ended. He sat in the silence, smiling to himself. He pushed his glasses back up his nose. Then he seemed to sense Dicey, silent in the doorway. He turned and looked at her.

"Who are you?" Dicey asked. "Are you the music teacher?"

"Isaac Lingerle," he said. He watched her watching him. "You must be Dicey."

"I didn't see any car," Dicey said.

"It's parked out front, under a big tree."

"What are you doing here?"

"I brought Maybeth home, and I want to ask your grandmother a question. But she said first Maybeth had to do some reading. That couldn't wait, she said. Your grandmother's not the woman to argue with."

At that, Dicey smiled. He smiled back at her.

"Maybeth has to work awfully hard," Dicey explained. "It's important for her."

"What about you, do you have to work hard?"

"Not at school," Dicey told him. "They'll be through pretty soon. I've gotta wash my hands to help get supper."

He turned back to the piano. His hands, poised above the keys, as if he was thinking about what to play. He was as massive as a mountain, Dicey thought. Or at least a big hill.

She was coming back downstairs, having dusted off her shorts and her shirt as well as washed her hands, when she met Gram. The woman went into the living room and waited for the music to break off.

Mr. Lingerle turned to face her and stood up. "Beethoven," he said, as if she'd asked him something.

"You're not married," Gram told him.

He looked puzzled, then his face turned a little pink. "As you see," he said.

"Then you'll stay for supper," Gram told him.

Dicey almost protested: they would never have enough food to fill that huge body.

"I don't know," he said. He looked uneasy, as if he didn't trust Gram.

"I've got no time to talk now, but after supper while Dicey does the dishes," Gram told him. She turned and left the room.

Dicey was laughing inside her head at the effect Gram always had on people. Mr. Lingerle stood looking at the place where Gram's bare feet had stood.

"How'd she know I wasn't married?" he demanded.

"She was asking you," Dicey said.

"That was a question?" He shook his head. "What a family," he remarked.

Dicey closed her mouth over her response and left him alone there.

They had crabs for dinner and baked potatoes. Gram told the boys to empty every crab they had into the bushel basket, and by the size of the mound of cooked crabs on the center of the table, Dicey could tell that Gram shared her estimate of Mr. Lingerle's appetite. James looked at their guest once, and then kept his eyes off him. Sammy tried not to stare and didn't succeed. Maybeth, looking tiny next to him, kept up a kind of chatter about school. Sometimes, if Mr. Lingerle asked him a direct question, Sammy talked too. Mr. Lingerle seemed to know Sammy. Mr. Lingerle ate only four crabs after all, just like Dicey, and he picked out the littlest potato when the plate came to him, and he had only a couple of slices of tomato.

Finally, Sammy couldn't keep his mouth shut any longer. "You don't eat very much," he accused the guest.

Mr. Lingerle flushed again. Dicey wondered about this, because he was entirely grown up and not even that young any more, not even a young grown-up. He took a deep breath and answered Sammy, and all the rest of them. "Let's just acknowledge that I'm fat."

"Nobody said anything," Gram snapped.

Mr. Lingerle drew back. "I just think it's better to say," he apologized.

"Well, you're right," she snapped. "On both counts."

Dicey giggled. She thought her grandmother was pretty funny sometimes. Dicey enjoyed her grandmother, and the way her grandmother's mind worked. Mr. Lingerle gave Dicey a curious look, and his eyes became less wary. "You Tillermans certainly take some getting used to," he remarked. "Maybeth has been surprise enough. I'm a simple man," he said, with a smile that creased the flesh around his mouth. "I'm planning to relax and enjoy myself, unless you object?"

"We want you to," Maybeth told him.

"*Did* you eat enough?" Sammy asked.

James tried to shush him, without success.

"Frankly, no. But here's what I'll do. When I get home, I'll stuff myself with something. I'm always nervous, the first time people meet me, and I'm never hungry when I'm nervous. Does that answer your question?"

"You count your blessings, young man," Gram said to Sammy; but her eyes were twinkling.

"Yes, Gram," he answered. "Next time I won't say anything."

"Good." Then Gram sent the little kids into the living room to do their homework. Dicey rolled up the crab shells in newspaper, washed and dried the dishes and glassware. She heard Mr. Lingerle ask Gram if Maybeth couldn't have two lessons a week instead of one. She heard Gram say no.

"Listen to me for a minute," Mr. Lingerle pleaded. "I'm not saying Maybeth is a genius, or anything like it. But she *is* one of those people, one of those lucky people, who will always have music in their lives. People who can always find pleasure in music, no matter what else—hurts them, or goes wrong. I'd like to give her as much music as I can, because—because I want to. It's a pleasure for me. And then—" his chair creaked as he leaned forward—"when I hear what the other teachers say about her—and when I see how hard she works—at the piano she has success. Don't you want her to be successful, somewhere?"

"Of course, we do," Gram snapped. Dicey, polishing plates dry, knew what was bothering Gram. Money. But Gram wasn't going to admit that. Dicey admired her pride, but she thought Gram was wrong not to tell Mr. Lingerle.

"I know what you're thinking, girl," Gram said. Dicey came to stand beside her.

"I'm right," Dicey said.

"You always think you're right," Gram said.

Dicey just went back to the sink. She could have been finished five minutes ago, but she wanted to listen in.

Gram was silent, then said, "We don't have the money."

"I wasn't asking for money," Mr. Lingerle cried, exasperated. "Did I mention money?"

Dicey turned around to catch the end of Gram's quick smile. "If you can afford it," Gram said.

"I can't afford not to," Mr. Lingerle told her. "I guess you can't know—how exhilarating it is to teach someone like Maybeth. So, we're agreed?"

"Entirely," Gram said.

Before he left, Mr. Lingerle played them all a couple of pieces on the piano. Then he asked them to sing for him, because Maybeth had told him they liked to sing, so they sang "Amazing Grace." Mr. Lingerle joined in with a rich bass harmony. Gram asked them to sing "Who Will Sing for Me," and they did. Then Sammy wanted to sing "The Old Lady Who Swallowed a Fly." When they had sung themselves out, Mr. Lingerle thanked them for a pleasant evening and left, getting himself, somehow, into a little Volkswagen that jounced off down the driveway, following its thin beams of light. They turned back to homework.

When Dicey was saying good night to Sammy, her brother said to her: "I didn't know he was like that."

"Like what?"

"Nice."

"What did you think he was like?"

"Funny." Sammy rolled over and looked at her with hazel eyes. "The kids all laugh at him."

"Because he's fat?"

He nodded.

"Do you?"

Sammy shrugged. "I've never been in trouble yet," he said.

Dicey finished her work apron the earliest of anyone in the home ec class. She spent the rest of the days assigned to this project pretending she still had work to do (so that Miss Eversleigh would keep off her back) and getting her other homework finished. On the day the project was due, Miss Eversleigh told every girl to put on her apron. Dicey stuck a marker in the story she was reading for English and jerked her apron over her head. She sat down again and opened her book.

But everybody had to stand up. Dicey wasn't sorry she'd done as bad a job as she'd done, but she wished she didn't have to stand up so everybody else could see. She made her face stony.

There was silence for a few minutes, while everybody looked at what everybody else had made (everybody except Dicey, who kept on reading), and Miss Eversleigh went around to everyone, like a general reviewing the troops, Dicey thought, acting as if the aprons mattered. When the first ripple of laughter began, Dicey looked up.

They were looking at her, at her apron. Well, she knew the hem rippled up and down, and the neckband pulled one side of the bib up to her shoulder, and the two big red buttons she'd used for decoration on the bib sat at just the wrong places. She knew that and she didn't care. She glared at the laughing faces, her chin high. Wilhemina was trying not to laugh, but her cheeks puffed out with holding it in, and her eyes glistened. Dicey just stared at her. The only other angry person in the room was Miss Eversleigh, and she was staring anger at Dicey. Dicey was thinking of what to say, and she kept her chin up like Gram's, when the bell rang. Ending class.

Dicey whipped her apron up over her head and rolled it into a ball. She grabbed her books, fast, because Miss Eversleigh was moving toward her. She rushed out of the room, slamming the apron into the trash basket by the door.

In the hall she collided with Mina. "What do *you* want," she demanded.

"It *was* funny-looking," Mina said.

"I wanted to take mechanical drawing," Dicey said. "If I were a boy, they'd have found room for me in that class." She heard the anger in her own voice.

"Don't take it out on me," Mina said, angry herself now. "Boy. I thought I could count on you not to be–ordinary."

"I never asked you to count on me for anything," Dicey said. She stormed down the hall, riding the waves of her own anger. At least it was Friday and she wouldn't have to go to school again until two days later.

When Dicey got home on Fridays, she usually had the house to herself for a few minutes. Gram picked Sammy up at school, and they did grocery shopping before returning together in the outboard. James was off delivering papers. Maybeth had her second piano lesson on Fridays.

Dicey slammed around the house, taking her books up to her room, pouring a glass of milk. She swept out the downstairs with quick strokes of the broom. She began to feel all right again. She was about to go out to the barn and get down to work, when Sammy and Gram arrived; so she went down through the marsh to the boat, to get the last bags of groceries.

"We're having steak tonight," Sammy announced. "Gram got it."

"Got the steak, and a check from Welfare," Gram said. Her mouth was tight. "They paid us everything from the time we first filed. So I thought–something to celebrate. If it deserves celebration."

Gram didn't like taking charity, Dicey knew that because Gram said so. For that matter, neither did she. But Gram had said, when she finally agreed to take them in, that that might be what they had to do.

"I must say," Gram said, moving from table to refrigerator, "I've never gotten money back on taxes before. It ought to feel good."

Dicey finished the sentence for her: But it doesn't. She felt like she ought to apologize to Gram. After all, it had been her idea to come down here and see if they could stay. The words *I'm sorry* started to form themselves on her lips. But nobody made Gram do things. If she didn't want the children, all she had to do was say so.

"Steak'll be good," was all Dicey said.

"It better be," Gram answered.

"I wanna play catch," Sammy said. "Dicey?"

She shook her head.

"Please?"

"James'll be home in a while. Ask him."

"Gram? Will you?"

"Not today." Gram was slamming around the kitchen. Dicey guessed she knew about how her grandmother felt.

"I'm gonna go meet James," Sammy decided. He ran out the door, letting it slam behind him. Gram had taken off her shoes and was putting eggs and butter out on the table. She hauled down her big mixing bowl. "What are you making?" Dicey asked.

"Chocolate cake and I don't want any help, nor need it," Gram said.

The last time they had Gram's chocolate cake was for Sammy's birthday; but then Gram seemed happy about making it.

Dicey went out to the barn. While she scraped, she thought about the English assignment. She'd show them she could write something good. She began thinking of how she would write about Momma, how to say enough for it to tell what had happened, but not as if she was talking about her own mother. After a while, she put down the scraper and went upstairs to the desk in her bedroom.

She had thought of a way to begin that would give her a good ending too. She began to write.

Downstairs, she heard the boys come in, with raised voices as if they were quarreling. Vaguely, she wondered what they could be quarreling about. Gram would settle it. Dicey continued writing, until a question that had been hovering around the back of her head, away behind her ideas, sneaked around to the front: wasn't Maybeth supposed to be home by now?

Outside, the sun was going down. Time to get to the kitchen, probably past time. Clouds crowded the sky, heavy and dark. The marsh lay under a pale mist, and in the distance, the Bay was dark purple.

James and Sammy sat over a game of checkers. Dickey said hello before turning down the hall to the kitchen. "I'd steer clear," James advised her. "Something's eating Gram."

"She got a welfare check today," Dicey explained.

"I don't know," James said.

Gram had set the table and put out glasses on the counter. She had put potatoes into the oven to bake. She had a stick of butter ready on the table. The cake she had made stood on the sideboard, tall and frosted. The steak waited beside a huge iron frying pan, beside the stove. Gram sat at the head of the table, in her usual place. Under the yellow kitchen light, her face looked pale and tired.

"And what do *you* want?" Gram demanded.

"I was going to set the table," Dicey said. Why was Gram angry at her? "Where's Maybeth?"

"Late," Gram said. Her face closed off.

"What were Sammy and James fighting about?" Dicey asked.

"The place of a perfectionist in this world," Gram said. Whatever that meant. "Ask 'em yourself."

Dicey went back down to the living room. "What *were* you two quarreling about?" she demanded.

"Are you angry?" Sammy asked. "Why is everyone angry at me?"

"Nothing really," James told her. His hazel eyes were worried.

"We shouldn't have bothered Gram. Sammy just said I wasn't being careful where I threw the papers, it wasn't even important."

"Were you?" Dicey asked him.

James shook his head.

"I told him," Sammy said.

"Do you think something's happened to Maybeth?" James asked.

"What could happen to Maybeth," Dicey said to soothe him. But, of course, anything could happen to Maybeth, or any of them, or anyone. James was too smart to be fooled about that, but he let himself believe her. She could see in his eyes how he was making himself believe her, and her tone of voice.

"Is that why Gram's angry?" Sammy asked.

Dicey began to understand. She looked out the front windows, past the wide porch and down to where the driveway disappeared into the narrow stand of pines. Nothing except growing darkness. "She really is late."

"I'm hungry," Sammy said.

Dicey wandered back down to the kitchen. Worry was like the mist along the marsh, it rose up from the floors of the house.

"What time does she usually get in?" Dicey asked Gram.

"An hour and more," Gram answered. "If you haven't got anything to do in here, why don't you just leave me alone."

Dicey obeyed. She was halfway down the hall when she met James and Sammy coming at her, both running. "The car's here!" Sammy called, as if Dicey were miles away.

Maybeth had burst into the kitchen and was explaining. Gram had a smile on her face that didn't flash away the way her smiles usually did. Mr. Lingerle climbed heavily up the steps and waited in the doorway, with the darkness behind him. He had a bandage on his right hand.

" . . . a flat tire," Maybeth was saying.

"That's all right," Gram said.

"And the jack slipped, and it caught his fingers, and somebody stopped to help us. We went to the Emergency Room."

Gram looked up. "Come on in, what's this Maybeth's telling me?"

"I'm so sorry, Mrs. Tillerman, I know you must have been worried. I tried to call from the hospital–"

"I don't have a phone," Gram told him.

"It wasn't even that serious, only a couple of stitches," he apologized.

"I don't have a phone and I should. With children in the house it's irresponsible not to have a phone," Gram said angrily.

"It's all right, Gram," Maybeth said. Gram reached out and hugged Maybeth close. Then she let her go and took a deep breath.

"Yes, it is, and I'll get a phone put in. You'll stay for supper," she asked. "We're having steak."

"Gram," Sammy protested. "*Gram.*"

She ignored him and waited for Mr. Lingerle's answer. Dicey understood, just then, and wished she didn't, just what the Tillermans had done to Gram by coming to live with her. Because she did love them, and that meant not only the good parts, but also the worry and fear. Until the children came along, nothing could hurt Gram. And now . . . but Gram must have known that, she'd had children of her own, she must have known that when she said they could live with her. Dicey wished she didn't understand. She wished she could still be like Sammy, concerned only about whether or not he'd have as much steak as he wanted, already forgetting the worry since everything was all right again.

"Thank you, I'd enjoy that," Mr. Lingerle said.

"Good," said Gram, with a quick glance at Sammy.

Sammy looked up at Mr. Lingerle. "Are you still nervous when you eat here?" he asked. His eyes shone hopefully.

Mr. Lingerle burst out laughing, and the Tillermans joined him.

Yolonda's Genius

Carol Fenner

—⋅❖ NEWBERY HONOR, 1996 ❖⋅—

ALTHOUGH HER FIRST-GRADE BROTHER, ANDREW, IS HAVING TROUBLE LEARNING TO READ, FIFTH-GRADER YOLONDA, BIG AND STRONG FOR HER AGE, IS CONVINCED THAT HE IS A MUSICAL GENIUS AND SETS OUT TO PROVE IT. BUT FIRST SHE HAS TO PROVE HER OWN SELF.

This is a new place, a strange place, Yolonda thought, and a part of her knew she was dreaming. There was something missing from this place in her dream. It was quiet all around and there was a fresh smell like parks in summer–Grant Park near the fountain when a breeze swept in cool off Lake Michigan. But this quiet didn't belong to Grant Park or any truly familiar place, and Yolonda felt a sadness seeping into her dreaming and realized she was waking up. And realized where she was.

She kept her eyes closed and willed herself back in Chicago, willed the lively noise from morning streets outside her Chicago window–garbage trucks clanking and the shouts of the workers, the rush and buzz of automobiles, the indistinct thumpings of the family in the next apartment. But the quiet of her dream stayed with her. It was so still that she could hear the birds outside.

The sadness stayed with her, too. So she lay there and waited for it to settle or go away. And while she waited, eyes closed, plump hands curved gently near her cheek, two comforting sounds filled the light spaces in the air. One was her ample stomach growling for breakfast. The other was the sweet sound of her little brother, Andrew, playing on his wooden pipe. He was piping his special waking-up music, a song he'd invented all by himself.

Yolonda's sadness began to ease away. She opened her eyes. It used to be her habit to sleep until she heard Andrew's music. The bright, clear notes had always been her alarm clock back home in Chicago. But ever since they'd moved away, months and months ago, it was her sadness that woke her first—that and the quiet.

Get up, get dressed, sang the sweet roll and pitch of Andrew's pipe. Yolonda sat up. Sunlight was spilling through the trees outside, making moving patterns on the floor of a room she didn't have to share. That was another thing. The morning light didn't stay in the squared-off patterns she'd taken for granted back home in Chicago. It moved all around, and the shadow shapes were soft and blurred, not clear and sharp.

Her mother said they'd all get used to Grand River, Michigan. But the new school still seemed unreal. It wasn't just the newer-looking fifth-grade textbooks—or the work. Some was easier, some tougher; some was just as boring. It would take longer than a few months for Yolonda, accustomed to scenting trouble, to relax. There was no trouble in the air in Grand River—at least no trouble that threatened her life or her lunch money. There was no trouble. There was no nuthin'.

Yolonda threw back the covers to air the bed while she dressed. Then she made it up carefully. Her momma said she made a mean bed.

She could hear her mother outside in the backyard, watering her new plantings. She was growing flowers in their wide, green, clean backyard. They had shade trees and a picnic table and a brand-new unchained barbecue grill. If Andrew left his bike outside, it was still there in the morning. You never needed to be on your toes in this town. Boring.

Before going downstairs to breakfast, Yolonda sneaked into her mother's room. It was a big bedroom with pretty new curtains and a picture view of the quiet street and the trees with their flutter of new spring leaves. Her mother had her own bathroom with peach-colored tiles and little round lights around the wide mirror. Back in Chicago their apartment had cost more and had only one bathroom.

"My money goes a lot further here in Grand River," Yolonda's momma said now every time she paid the rent. "That's another plus for this town."

Yolonda's eight-dollar allowance went further in Grand River, too. She had tried to work a cost-of-living increase out of her momma during the confusion of moving four months ago, but her momma had just raised her eyebrows and then laughed. "Trying to take advantage of your poor, broke momma? You are one smart girl, Yolonda. But your momma's still smarter. You should be getting a *decrease* for this town." Yolonda had quickly dropped the subject.

On the peach-colored bathroom counter were her momma's creams and powders, her perfumed soaps and colognes. Yolonda carefully opened a blue jar of moisturizer and dabbed some on her face, then smoothed it in.

She'd started primping back in Chicago when she'd begun to fall in love with Tyrone and dream about the bright glint of his eyes. Once he'd commented, "You sure smell good, Londa," and she had savored his voice, that moment, the high shine of his eyes for weeks.

Now she reached for her mother's Giorgio. The perfume cost a hundred seventy dollars an ounce, so her mother only bought the cologne. Yolonda dabbed some on her handkerchief to run on her throat later. She stuffed the handkerchief into her backpack. Her mother would freak out if she smelled it on her. The cologne itself cost forty bucks. *Poor broke Momma—yeah.*

Even though the Tyrone she'd been so crazy about was gone from her life, the habits of attracting him remained. Besides, in this nerdy hick school, she was establishing her image of worldly superiority. Giorgio helped.

As she descended the stairs, the rich smell of bacon filled her nostrils. Good, thought Yolonda. She loved bacon—and the thick smell would cancel any traces of Giorgio.

Andrew was already at the kitchen table, sitting with his back to the sun, which, softened by breezy curtains, spilled into the room. He looked like a thin little angel to Yolonda. He was listening intently to something. Their mother, an apron over her business suit, was turning the sizzling bacon. And there were pancakes browning on the griddle.

Andrew picked up his ever-present harmonica and played a strange buzzing, cracking sound, his cheeks puffing out like plums.

"What's that?" asked Yolonda as she shoved herself into a chair.

"The bacon," said Andrew, a little indignant that she hadn't recognized the sound of bacon on his harmonica.

"Oh, yeah. Yeah. I see," said Yolonda. Now that he'd named it, the sound *did* have the sizzle of bacon. Like some paintings didn't make sense until you read the title.

"Now I'm trying to hear the pancakes," said Andrew.

"You can stop playing, Andrew," said their mother, placing plates before each of them. "You can start eating."

No one had to tell Yolonda to start. The rich scent of almond flavoring rose with the heat from pancakes browned in beautiful patterns. She already knew she wanted seconds before she even started on firsts.

"No seconds, Yolonda," said her mother, reading her mind. "And see that Andrew eats his. I'm already late."

As her mother hurried out the door to her car, she hollered back. "Make sure he eats, Yolonda. Don't you eat his breakfast for him."

"All right!" Yolonda yelled back in her meanest voice. Her mother was in too big a hurry to challenge her rudeness now. Yolonda decided not to tell her that she was still wearing her apron.

Anyway, Andrew wouldn't eat his pancakes, and Yolonda wasn't about to let them go to waste.

They waited for the school bus at their corner. Each morning Yolonda steeled herself for the ride. She hadn't yet figured out how to handle these whispering girls or the sniggering boys with their stage-whisper slurs about her big body. The taunts came from black kids as well as white kids.

Back in Chicago, most of the kids in her school, in her neighborhood, were black. Everyone had learned not to name-call or bait her. Even older boys steered clear. But that was in the freedom of the street, where Yolonda could unleash her sharp tongue and use her powerful arms, her great size, to scare off any abuse.

Here you had to be careful. The bus driver could turn you in for fighting. The atmosphere, with more white kids than black, was tame and murky. Yolonda studied it carefully.

So far, she had kept to herself. She read on the bus, ignoring "Hey, whale, you'll break the seat," hurled like a blade from behind. She made her silence a brick wall and kept on reading. She reviewed last night's homework or buried herself in a novel, but a part of her mind noted who the offender was. *You wait*, said that part of her mind to comfort her. *You wait.*

This morning she realized with dismay that, in her guilty rush to finish the rest of Andrew's pancakes, she had left *Island of the Blue Dolphins* on a chair.

Well, she could look over her homework. She always did her homework. Being a good student was easier in Grand River than in Chicago. You didn't have to camouflage being school-smart here. In Chicago it was uncool to get good grades—not a black thing. *Who you think you are?*

When the bus came, she had her homework out of her backpack. The seats up front were occupied, and she didn't want to push down the narrow aisle past everyone to the seats in the back. The maniacs sat in the back. She decided to stand. This bus driver was easygoing; he might not make her sit if she was quiet.

There was a small space on one seat near the window, and she said gruffly to Andrew, "Sit." Clutching his harmonica, her brother eased over a third grader and sat.

Yolonda stood holding on to the edge of a seat in the second row. She held her homework toward the light, the better to read her pretty, slanted handwriting. She dotted her *i*'s with tiny circles and ended every sentence in a curled sweep.

"Sit down, whale. You're breakin' the floor," a voice hissed at her from somewhere midbus. Gasps, giggles, and guffaws erupted around her. Yolonda straightened her back, keeping her eyes on her homework. Her mind searched the boys' voices she knew. White boy, definitely. Was it dumb George? Was it Danny with his daddy longlegs and pimpled cheeks? Gerard, smart and sly in his too-white shirt?

"Hey, whale!"

Whales surfaced in Yolonda's mind. *Their big gray heads were slapped by little waves, their small eyes peering.*

Yolonda turned her face toward the voice. Danny-longlegs still had his hand cupped around his mouth, his legs splayed out in the aisle.

Slowly Yolonda edged her way back to his seat. He sat slumped, with a smirk on his face, long legs hogging the narrow space.

"What do you know about whales, blisterface?" asked Yolonda softly. She looked down at him. "You don't know diddly, do you?"

Danny shifted uneasily in his seat, but slid an angry glance at her.

The whales peered from their little eyes. Then they sprouted up beautiful gushes of water like the fountain in Grant Park.

Yolonda looked into Danny's reddening face. "Whales are the most remarkable mammals in the ocean—all five oceans."

Danny's lip curled, but before he could make any reply, Yolonda carefully lifted her solid right foot and brought it squarely and gently down over Danny-longleg's huge running shoe. She watched his face pale under the frozen smirk as she slowly settled her weight onto his foot.

"Whales sing to one another through hundreds of miles of water. They have a high keening sound and a low dirgelike sound."

"Get off my effin' foot, you cow," muttered Danny through his teeth. There was a giggle from behind them.

"Right," said Yolonda, her voice gooey with mock praise, "the female whale is called a cow. Didn't know a farmer boy like you was so well informed." And Yolonda leaned her weight deeper into his foot.

He grimaced in pain and shot a glance at the bus driver.

"The music whales make is found to be beautiful, and people make recordings of it. It is found to be powerful, and musicians create background music for it."

His face went blank and she knew she was mesmerizing him. She knew he didn't want to sound stupid in front of his friends and the girls in back. She knew a struggle against her foot would look uncool.

She increased the pressure on his toes by twisting away from him and pretending to review her homework again.

"Get off my effin' foot!" His anger had a begging sound, and Yolonda was gratified by loud giggling and snorts of laughter from the back of the bus.

"Keep it down to a dull roar, kids," the bus driver called good-naturedly without taking his eyes off the road.

The whales sank, lifting their tails high above the water like a signal. Deep in the ocean, their voices sent out a high swelling cry, sharing their message of victory for a hundred miles.

Although she was prepared to confront Danny-longlegs when the bus reached the school, he brushed past her in a hurry, heading for his room.

Yolonda watched Andrew trudge off to his first-grade class, slipping his harmonica into his back pocket. Andrew didn't do well in school like Yolonda. He couldn't even read one word yet and had to attend a special reading class for slow learners. He didn't make friends easily, but he didn't make enemies either.

"Oh, that was really cool." The voice at her elbow was manlike, gruff. When she turned, Yolonda was surprised to find herself looking down into a small, pale girl's face.

"Hi. I'm Shirley Piper," said the man voice. All of this Shirley person was small except for her voice and her large, pale blue eyes whirling behind the thickest glasses Yolonda had ever seen— whirling, yes, and twitching behind the thick lenses.

"You were really something," said the Shirley person. "What else do you do?" Then she laughed a kind of deep, dry ha-ha-ha-hacking laugh.

"I play the piano," said Yolonda demurely, "mostly classical like Mozart. I get straight A's." She stared at the Shirley person. "I look after my kid brother. I do the laundry for our whole family. I can make cake from scratch."

Then Yolonda decided to lie. "I do double Dutch." She watched Shirley's face for traces of disbelief. None. "I can do 'Teddy Bear.' And 'Pepper'—with the right rope turners, of course."

Shirley Piper's eyes whirled admiringly. "That bit about the whales. I loved the narrative you gave Danny about the whales. Did you memorize it or are you a genius?"

"No," said Yolonda. She was surprised at the word *narrative*. "I didn't really memorize that. I just *knew* it." She could barely re-member what she'd said to Danny-longlegs—just the image in her head of majestic whales. She checked Shirley out again. "What do *you* do?" she asked.

"Oh, I don't have all your talents," said Shirley in her gruff voice. "I read a lot, but I barely find enough time to study. My A's aren't straight. More like crooked A's. They sort of hump over the B's and a C or two." She ha-ha'd again. "I can't even turn the ropes for double Dutch."

"Don't feel bad," said Yolonda, suddenly generous. "Turning the ropes correctly is an art—it's really hard."

The bell rang and they both turned hurriedly toward the school.

"You have to have good rhythm and your partner has to be in sync with you. You know, really good vibes," hollered Yolonda after Shirley's scurrying figure. Without looking around, the Shirley per-son flapped her hand in a wave.

Well, I've impressed one person in this burg at least, thought

Yolonda, even if she has a man voice and whirlygig eyes. Even if she is whiter than white.

She only felt slightly guilty about her lie. She was sure that she could do "Teddy Bear" here among these countrified kids. It looked a lot slower and easier. They didn't know diddly about double Dutch in this burg, even though they worked at it. She'd seen black girls here teaching white girls "the ropes." She wasn't sure black people and white people could get it together right. And no one here did it like they did back on the streets of Chicago. No one could fly in and out of the whirr-slap of ropes like the Chicago girls, who had never been her friends, who hardly ever let her turn the ropes. No one here had such quick, light feet and legs like hot motor pistons. Yolonda had to admit to herself that "Pepper" was too wildly fast anywhere for someone her size to master. That was a bigger lie.

She'd told another sort-of lie to the Shirley person. She'd never had good enough vibes with anyone to turn the ropes in perfect rhythm. She was always criticizing her partner before they even started. "You're too short," or, belligerently, "You never done this before?"

Only once had she seen rope turning done in perfect sync. In Chicago. On the playground at recess. The girls had been close in size and they moved their arms in an easy, relaxed way—turning, turning, their eyes fixed, not on each other, but sort of out of focus, listening—the way Andrew did all the time. When the recess bell had rung, the partners had laughed and slapped gently at each other with pleasure, then wound up the ropes. They had gone back into the school building with their arms slung across each other's shoulders.

For a while, Yolonda liked to remember that. She liked to pretend that those girls had been her friends.

The View from Saturday

E. L. Konigsburg

—∶ NEWBERY MEDAL, 1997 ∶—

NADIA DIAMONDSTEIN IS ONE OF FOUR BRILLIANT, SHY NEW YORK STU-
DENTS WHO IS CHOSEN TO REPRESENT THE EPIPHANY MIDDLE SCHOOL
SIXTH-GRADE CLASS IN AN ACADEMIC BOWL COMPETITION. SHE ANSWERS
THE QUESTION "WHAT IS THE NAME GIVEN TO THAT PORTION OF THE NORTH
ATLANTIC OCEAN THAT IS NOTED FOR ITS ABUNDANCE OF SEAWEED, AND
WHAT IS ITS IMPORTANCE TO THE ECOLOGY OF OUR PLANET?"

NADIA TELLS OF TURTLE LOVE

My grandfather is a slim person of average height with heavy, heath-
ery-gray eyebrows. He lives in a high-rise condominium on the beach
in Florida. He lives there with his new wife whom he calls Margy. I was
told to call her Margaret, not Aunt Margaret or Mrs. Diamondstein. It
sounded disrespectful to me–calling a woman old enough to be my
grandmother by her first name, but I did as I was told.

Last summer, just before my grandfather married Margaret,
my mother and father got divorced, and Mother moved the two of

us to upstate New York where she had grown up. She said that she needed some autumn in her life. I had never thought that I would see autumn in New York or anywhere else because even when we vacationed at a place that had one, we always had to return for school before it started. In Florida school starts before Labor Day. Whatever it says on the calendar, Florida has de facto summer.

Dividing up my time was part of the divorce settlement. I was to spend Thanksgiving, spring vacation, and one month over the summer with Dad. He left Christmas holidays for Mother because it is her holiday, not his. I am the product of a mixed marriage.

This first summer of their separation, Dad chose August for his visitation rights. He picked us up early Friday evening. *Us* means Ginger and me. Ginger is my dog. I do not know who was happier to see me at the airport–Dad or Ginger. The worst part of the trip had been checking Ginger into the baggage compartment.

Dad always was a nervous person, but since the divorce he had become terminally so. He was having a difficult time adjusting to being alone. He had sold the house that we lived in when we were a family and had moved into a swinging singles apartment complex, but my father could no more swing than a gate on rusty hinges.

For the first day and a half after I arrived, Dad hovered over me like the Goodyear blimp over the Orange Bowl. He did not enjoy the hovering, and I did not enjoy being hovered, but he did not know what to do with me, and I did not know what to tell him, except to tell him to stop hovering, which seemed to be the only thing he knew how to do.

On Sunday we went to see Grandpa Izzy and Margaret.

Grandpa Izzy was happy to see me. Under those bushy eyebrows of his, Grandpa Izzy's eyes are bright blue like the sudden underside of a bird wing. His eyes have always been the most alive part of him, but when Bubbe Frieda died, they seemed to die, too. Since he married Margaret though, they seem bright enough to give off light of their own. He is sixty-nine years old, and he is in love.

Margaret is a short blonde. She is very different from my bubbe but not very different from the thousands who make their home in South Florida. There are so many blond widows in the state of Florida, and they are all so much alike, they ought to have a kennel breed named and registered for them. Like all the others, Margaret dresses atrociously. She wears pastel-colored pantsuits with elastic waists or white slacks with overblouses of bright, bold prints. She carries her eyeglasses—blue-rimmed bifocals—on a gold metal chain around her neck. They all do. Margaret is not fat, but she certainly is not slim. She is thick around the middle, and when she wears her green polyester pantsuit, she looks like a Granny Smith apple. Grandpa Izzy would say Delicious.

Grandpa Izzy and Margaret are like Jack-Sprat-could-eat-no-fat and his wife-could-eat-no-lean. Grandpa Izzy says that Margaret is *zaftig*, which is Yiddish for pleasingly plump. Everything about her pleases him. He seems to find it difficult to keep himself from pinching her or pinching himself for having had the good fortune to find and marry her. Such public displays of affection can be embarrassing to a prepubescent girl like me who is not accustomed to being in the company of two married people who like each other.

On Sunday we went out for brunch at one of those mammoth places where the menu is small and portions are large, and every senior citizen leaves with a Styrofoam box containing leftovers. We had to wait to be seated at the restaurant because Sunday brunch is a major social custom in Florida retirement communities. Dad twice asked the restaurant hostess how much longer we would have to wait. Grandpa Izzy and Margaret tried to tell Dad that they did not mind waiting since visiting with each other was part of the plan, and they did not mind doing it at the restaurant. But hovering at low altitudes seemed to be my father's new best thing.

When we were finally seated, we had a nice enough time. Margaret had Belgian waffles and did not require a Styrofoam box for leftovers because there were none; she ate everything that was on her plate—strawberry preserves, pseudo whipped cream and all. She did not order decaf coffee but drank three cups of regular.

Margaret was not at all curious about me. I thought she would want to know how I liked our new home, which is in Epiphany, the very town she had lived in before she moved to Florida. Maybe she thought I was not curious about her because I did not ask her about her wedding, which neither Mother nor I attended. But I believe that the grown-up should ask the questions first, and besides, Mother and I had gotten a full report on the wedding from Noah Gershom, who, due to unforeseen circumstances, had been best man. I did not find Noah's account of the events surrounding his becoming best man quite as amusing as he did, but for several complicated reasons, I did not express my opinion.

One of the complications was that my mother works for Dr. Gershom, who is Noah's father. My mother is a dental hygienist by profession, and Dr. Gershom is a dentist. One of the reasons we moved to Epiphany was that Mother got a job there. My mother happens to be an excellent hygienist, and Dr. Gershom was lucky to get her, but nevertheless, I thought it best not to tell Noah Gershom that his account of my grandfather's wedding was not as amusing as he thought it was.

Dad's new apartment complex was miles away from our old neighborhood. I called two of my former friends, but getting together with them was not easy. Our schedules, which had once matched, seemed to be in different time zones now. Geography made the difference.

When we finally got together, I thought we would have fun. We did not. Either I had changed, or they had changed, or all of us did. I would not try again. I concluded that many friendships are born and maintained for purely geographical reasons. I preferred Ginger.

Work seemed to be the only thing that held Dad together, but leaving me alone that week while he went to the office made him feel guilty and ended up making him even more nervous, if such a thing were possible. I spent part of my time at the apartment complex pool, which was almost empty during the day. I read and watched talk shows and took Ginger on walks around the golf course that bordered the swinging singles complex. I enjoyed not having Dad hover over me, but I did not tell him so.

Grandpa Izzy called every day. He volunteered to come to swinging singles to pick me up after Dad left for work and after the morning rush-hour traffic. All the retirees in South Florida wait for the rush-hour traffic to be over, so that when they go out on the highways, they can create their own rush hour. But I declined. Then on Thursday, after I had had the unsatisfactory visit with my former friends, Grandpa Izzy called with a different suggestion. He asked Dad to drop me off at their place in the morning before he went to work. Margaret's grandson Ethan, who was my age, had arrived, and Grandpa Izzy thought a visit would be good for both of us. I thought he meant Ethan and me, but maybe he meant Dad and me because after he took the call, the look on my father's face was a new way to spell relief.

My only requirement was that I be allowed to bring Ginger. A lot of retirement high-rises have rules against dogs, visiting or otherwise, and I did not know Margaret's position on dogs. Grandpa Izzy said that Ginger would not be a problem. Of course, she never was. Ginger is a genius.

I did not know if I was developing an interest in boys, or if I would have washed my hair and put on my new blouse anyway. Perhaps, I was leaving prepubescence and was entering full pubescence or, perhaps, I was simply curious about Ethan. For example, why had Margaret said nothing about his coming when we had seen each other at Sunday's brunch? Margaret had mentioned having a grandson who was my age, but she said very little about him. Most grandmothers of her species carry a coffee-table-sized photo album in their tote-bag-sized pocketbooks. Either Margaret was a rare subspecies of grandmother or her grandson Ethan had done something strange to his hair. When grandmothers disapprove of grandsons, it is usually their hair. Their hair or their music. Or both. She must have known about his visit for at least two weeks because everybody I know has to buy airline tickets that far in advance to get the discount.

Grandpa Izzy's high-rise retirement condominium was three towns north of Dad's swinging singles apartment complex. The highway between them is bumper to bumper. Dad misjudged the time it would take to get there, so we did not arrive until after they had left for their morning walk. Dad gave me a key. I let myself in. There was a note on the refrigerator door saying that they had gone for their turtle walk and to make myself at home. The note was in Margaret's handwriting. No mistaking her *u*'s for *n*'s or her *i*'s for *e*'s. Margaret's handwriting was the smooth, round style used by the older generation of schoolteachers, which is exactly what Margaret was before she became an elementary school principal, which is what she was before she retired.

Ginger and I waited on the balcony and watched the three of them approach. Ethan appeared to be almost as tall as Margaret and almost as blond, but not for the same reason. From the distance of the balcony—it was the third floor—he appeared to be a healthy prepubescent. Of course, except for my father, appearances do not always tell much about a person's nervous condition.

The three of them were very excited when they returned.

Even though Ethan is Margaret's grandson, it was Grandpa who introduced me because Margaret did not. She went straight to the desk to dig a record book out of the drawer. "Ethan's lucky," Grandpa said. "Only his second day here, and this evening, we will be digging out one of our nests."

He was talking about turtle nests. Turtles had brought Grandpa and Margaret together.

• • •

The year after Bubbe Frieda had died, Grandpa Izzy sold their little house and moved to Century Village. For the next two years, early every morning, before the day got too hot, he drove to the beach where he took a walk. Many people from Century Village walked the beach where there was a sidewalk with markers for every half mile. A year ago last spring he noticed a blond *zaftig* woman who was returning about the same time he was leaving, so he began starting out earlier and earlier until, one day, they started out together. He introduced himself and asked her if she would like to take a walk with him. She replied by inviting him to join her on her turtle walk.

He accepted, not even knowing where or what it was.

And they have been doing it together ever since.

Margaret was checking in her record book. "We moved one hundred seven eggs," she said.

"We feel very protective of the nests we move," Grandpa explained to Ethan, who nodded as if he understood what Grandpa was talking about, leading me to believe that they had already explained turtles to him.

Sea turtles need beaches, of which Florida has many miles. All up and down the coastline, female turtles come out of the ocean and paddle their way across the sand, dig a hole, and lay eggs–about a hundred at a time. They use their flippers first to dig the hole and then to scoop the sand back over it before returning to the sea. The female will lay three to five clutches of eggs during a season, return to the water, and not come out of the water again for two or three years, when she is ready to lay again.

About fifty-five days after being laid, the eggs hatch.

From the first of May when the first eggs get laid until Halloween night when the last of them hatches, turtle patrols walk assigned stretches of beach. Members of a turtle patrol are trained to recognize the flipper marks that the mother turtles make.

About half the time the mother turtle lays her eggs in a dangerous place—where the eggs might get washed out because they are within the high tide line or where they might get trampled by people or run over by cars. Turtle eggs are a gourmet feast to birds, big fish, and especially raccoons. People approved by the Department of Environmental Protection are allowed to move the nests to safer ground. They post a stake with a sign over all the nests they find—the ones they move and the ones they do not—saying that it is against the law to disturb the nest. If you do, you can be fined up to $50,000 and/or go to jail for a year. The signs, which are bright yellow, make it very clear that it is an *and/or* situation.

Loggerheads are a threatened species. That means that they are not as seriously missing as endangered, but almost. Last year, encouraged by Grandpa Izzy, I did my science report on Florida turtles. We studied together. We accompanied Margaret on her turtle walks. (I called her Mrs. Draper then. I never guessed that only months later we would become almost related.) I got an A; Grandpa got permitted. Margaret had been permitted when they met.

I saved my report. I had begun it by asking, "Do you think it is harder to name Mr. Walter Disney's Seven Dwarfs or to name all five of the species of turtles that migrate off the coast of Florida?" My grandfather thought that was a wonderful way to begin a report. I had drawn a cover that showed all five kinds (loggerheads, greens, leatherbacks, hawksbill, and Kemp's ridley). My teacher commented on my cover, saying that it was exceptional. I saved the report because I thought I would draw a different cover—one showing a map of Florida beaches—and use it again in sixth grade when we were required to do a Florida history report. I did not know then that when I started sixth grade, I would be living in the state of divorce and New York.

Grandpa Izzy said, "Why don't you stay, Nadia? You've always enjoyed watching a nest being dug out. Ethan's coming." He looked over at Ethan, inviting him to reinforce the invitation. Ethan nod-ded slightly. "It'll be like old times," Grandpa said.

How could my Grandpa Izzy even begin to think that our dig-ging out a nest would be like old times? In old times, which were not so very long ago, I would have enjoyed—even been excited about—digging out a turtle nest. In old times Margaret would still be Mrs. Draper, and I would neither know nor care that she had a grandson Ethan.

"When will this happen?" I asked.

"After sunset, as usual," Grandpa replied, looking at me curi-ously, for he knew I knew.

"Oh, that is too bad," I said. "Dad is picking me up before sup-per, and he will be disappointed if I do not eat with him."

Grandpa said that he would call Dad at work and have him stop over so that he, too, could watch. And before I could tell them the real truth—that I would rather not attend at all—they had Dad on the telephone and everything was arranged. I was not angry, but I was seriously annoyed.

That afternoon the four of us went to the pool. I had to leave Ginger back at the apartment because dogs were not allowed at poolside. I had not brought my bathing suit, so I had to sit by the pool while the others swam. Margaret said that she was sorry that she did not have a bathing suit to lend me. "I don't think mine will fit," she said. I think she was attempting to make a joke because she smiled when she said it.

I do not know who, besides Margaret herself, any bathing suit of hers would fit. She had what the catalogs call "a mature figure," and she was not at all self-conscious about it or the starbursts of tiny blue veins on both her inner and outer thighs. Bubbe Frieda had never been *zaftig*, but she had the good taste to wear what is called "a dressmaker bathing suit." It had a little skirt and a built-in bra. Of course, my bubbe's bathing suit never got wet, and Margaret did forty-two laps.

Ethan practiced a few dives. Grandpa coached him. Then they came and sat by me. I was curious to know if Ethan's trip had been planned long before they announced it. I asked him if he had changed planes in Atlanta. He said that he had. "On my flight out of Atlanta, there were seven unaccompanied minors," I said.

He smiled. "There were only five on mine. I guess I was a little late in the season."

"Did you have an advance reservation?" I asked.

"Yes," he replied. "Why do you ask?"

"I was just wondering," I said. I did not tell him what I was wondering about. "When you travel with a pet," I added, "you must plan in advance. The worst part of my trip was worrying about Ginger. She had to fly as baggage. We were advised to tranquilize her and put her in a dog carrier. Ginger had never been tranquilized before, and she has been dopey all week. She is just now getting back to her real self. I promised her that I will not do that again."

"How will you get her back?"

"I am going to talk to her and tell her to be quiet so that I do not have to tranquilize her."

"Maybe you just gave her too strong a dose."

"Maybe. But I do not care to experiment. She will make the trip just fine. Ginger is a genius."

"Someone has written a book about the intelligence of animals. Border collies are smartest."

"Ginger would not be listed. She is a mixed breed. Like me."

"What's your mix?"

"Half-Jewish, half-Protestant."

"That's good," he said. "Like corn. It's called hybrid vigor."

I took that as a compliment, but I did not thank him for it. "Are you a hybrid?" I asked.

"Not at all. The only claim my family has to hybridization is right there," he said, pointing to Margaret. "Grandma Draper is a thoroughbred Protestant, and Izzy is a thoroughbred Jew. But they don't plan on breeding."

I think I blushed.

Margaret was in charge of fifteen permitted volunteers. That meant that if she could not do the turtle patrol, one of them could. Permitted volunteers were licensed to move a nest or dig out a nest after the eggs had hatched, but they had to be supervised by her. All fifteen of Margaret's permitteds, plus friends and other interested parties showed up for the digging out. As soon as other beach walkers saw the hovering over the nest, they joined in. The audience was enthusiastic. They ooohed and aaahed, and at least once every three minutes, one way or another, someone said that nature was wonderful. Four people said, "Fascinating." Ethan did not oooh or aaah, and he did not say fascinating. He watched as patiently as a cameraman from *National Geographic.* My father hovered with the rest of them and said "fascinating" twice. Hovering had become his great recreational pastime.

Turtle patrols keep very close watch on all the nests on their stretches of beach, and they know when they are ripe for hatching, and sometimes they are lucky enough to be there when the turtle nests are emerging. That is what a hatching is called. When the turtles push their way out of the sand and start waddling toward the water's edge, they look like a bunch of wind-up toys escaped from Toys "R" Us. Watching a nest hatch is more interesting than digging one out after they've hatched, which is really only a matter of keeping inventory and making certain that everything that was or is living is cleared out. During old times, I had ooohed and aaahed at the digging out, but that evening it seemed as exciting as watching a red light change.

Like a proud parent, Margaret watched as Grandpa Izzy dug out the nest. Wearing a rubber glove on his hand, he reached down into the nest as far as his arm pit. He removed:

96 empty egg shells

4 unhatched whole eggs

1 dead hatchling

3 turtles that were half-in/half-out of the shell but were dead.
  Those are called dead-pipped.

1 turtle that was half-in/half-out of the shell but was alive.
  Those are called live-pipped.

2 live ones

Margaret took notes, counted again, and said at last that it all added up.

Grandpa released the two live turtles onto the sand. Everyone lined up on either side of them as they made their way to the water's edge.

Turtles almost always hatch at night, and after they do, they head toward the light. Normally, the light they head for is the horizon on the ocean. However, if a hotel or high-rise along the ocean leaves its lights on, the turtles will head toward the brighter light of civilization and never make it to the ocean. They do not find food, and they die. Turtles are not trainable animals. Their brains are in the range of mini to micro.

When the two hatchlings reached the water, everyone along the parade route applauded, and my father said fascinating for the third time.

Back at the nest, Margaret examined the live-pipped. She announced, "I've decided to keep it." Judge, jury, and defending attorney.

Dad asked what would happen to it, and Margaret explained, "It'll take a few days to straighten itself out. We'll give it a safe, cool, dark place in the utility room and release it after sunset when it's ready."

Dad could have asked me. I did get an A on that report.

When baby turtles come out of their shells, which are round— about the same size as a golf ball—they are squinched up into a round shape that fits inside the eggs. After they break through the shell, they spend three days down in the sand hole straightening themselves out. Sometimes they die before they make it out of the shell. Those are the dead-pipped. They are counted and discarded with the unhatched and the empties. A permitted person has to decide if the live-pipped are more alive than dead. If the decision is that they stand a good chance of surviving, they need care. They are lifted from the nest and taken home and given shelter until they straighten themselves out, and then they are released onto the sand.

"We never carry them to the water," Margaret explained. "They must walk across their native sand. We think that something registers in their brains that kicks in twenty-five years later because they return to the beach where they were born to lay their eggs."

As Margaret was explaining this, I thought about my mother's returning to New York. Her birthday is September 12, and I wondered if her need to return to autumn in New York had anything to do with some switch that had been turned on when she emerged.

Back at the condo, Grandpa carried the bucket containing the live-pipped into the utility room, and we all sat down to have milk and cookies. Oreos. Bubbe would have had homemade ruggelach. Margaret did not even know what ruggelach were until Grandpa Izzy took her to a kosher delicatessen and introduced her to them. She already knew about bagels because bagels have become popular even in places that never heard of them.

Margaret liked ruggelach, but I could tell she had no intention of learning how to make them. Grandpa Izzy, who had enjoyed ruggelach and bobka as much as anyone, had adjusted to Entenmann's and Oreos. I asked Ethan if he knew ruggelach. He did not. Knowing ruggelach is a hybrid advantage.

Before the evening was over, Grandpa Izzy suggested that Dad bring me back early enough so that I could take the morning turtle walk with him and Margaret and Ethan.

Then Margaret said, "Allen, why don't you come, too? The exercise will be good for your foot." Dad had broken his foot on the day of their wedding, and it had not yet healed. Margaret believed that a bad mental attitude had slowed it down. Much to my surprise, Dad agreed. "What about Ginger?" I asked.

"No problem," Grandpa Izzy said. "Just keep her on a leash like old times."

I started to say that Ginger has grown to hate the leash, but once again a look on Dad's face told me something, and I said nothing. So it was from a look of Dad's and a sentence left unspoken that the sequel to the turtle habit got started.

Dad and I would leave his apartment early, meet Margaret, Grandpa, and Ethan on the beach, and do our walk. Then Dad would return to Grandpa's and change into his business suit and leave for work. If time permitted, Dad would join us for breakfast. If not, the four of us would eat without him. We usually watched the *Today Show* before going for a swim.

Grandpa and Ethan got into an unofficial contest about how many laps they could do. I did not participate. I took a short swim, got out of the water, sat on the sidelines and read while Grandpa was teaching Ethan how to dive. He wanted to teach me, too, but I preferred not to.

One afternoon, we went to the movies. It was blazing hot and bright outside. We went into the movies where it was cool and dark, and then we came back out into the bright, hot sun. I felt as if I had sliced my afternoon into thirds, like a ribbon sandwich. Ethan, who never said much, had a lot to say about the camera angles and background music and described the star's performance as subtle. Never before in all my life had I heard a boy use the word subtle.

Dad had tickets for *The Phantom of the Opera*. This was the real Broadway show except that it was the road company. Not knowing that Ethan would be visiting, he had bought only four. As soon as he found out that Ethan would be in town, he started calling the ticket office to buy one more, but there were none to be had. He kindly volunteered to give up his ticket, but Grandpa Izzy and Margaret would not hear of it. Margaret said that she would stay home, and Grandpa Izzy said that he didn't want to go if she didn't.

I expected Ethan to do the polite thing and say that he would stay home. But he did not. Of course, Ethan usually said nothing. Even when it was appropriate to say something, Ethan could be counted on to say nothing. But on the subject of who should give up a ticket, Ethan was particularly silent, which was a subtle hint that he really wanted to go. At the very last minute, the problem was solved. One of Dad's clients mentioned that he had an extra ticket, and Dad bought it from him on the spot.

We met at the theater. Ethan had insisted upon taking the odd seat, saying that he would be fine. The odd seat was three rows in front of ours and closer to the center of the stage, but I do not think Ethan knew it at the time. I think he wanted to be alone, or, I should say, without us. At intermission, Ethan bought one of the ten-dollar souvenir programs, and after the show he thanked my father at least five times for getting him a ticket.

Dad was pleased with the way the evening had turned out. We went to the Rascal House for ice-cream sundaes after the show. Ethan could hardly keep himself from thumbing through his ten-dollar program. His head must have stayed back at the theater long after we left, for when the waitress asked for his order, he said, "They must have more trapdoors on that stage than a magic act."

My father actually hummed as he looked over the menu, and then right after we placed our orders, he dropped his bombshell.

He asked Margaret if he could be listed on her permit. He would like to be able to substitute for her or Grandpa Izzy. His apartment house was not far from a beach, he explained, and he would transfer to someone's permit there after I went back north. Then he would like to train so that he could head up a turtle patrol. His goal was to get licensed.

"Like father, like son," he said, patting Grandpa Izzy on the back.

Margaret said, "We'll get the process started tomorrow." She must have been quite proud of her loggerheads. They got her my grandpa, and now they got her my dad.

I did not care. I had Ginger. I preferred animals with fur and some measure of intelligence. Ginger had grown sleek and muscular with our long turtle walks. She was more affectionate than ever. For example, when we got back to the apartment after *The Phantom of the Opera,* she greeted me as if I were the best friend she had ever had.

Inside me there was a lot of best friendship that no one but Ginger was using.

The day after Dad dropped his bombshell, he and Ethan, Margaret and Grandpa walked the beach together, a tight, three-generation foursome. They got ahead of Ginger and me, and I made no effort to catch up. Instead, I slowed down and walked at the water's edge so that I could kick at the waves as they rolled ashore. Ginger and I fell farther and farther behind the others. I saw Ethan stop to wait for Ginger and me to catch up. He did not call to us, and I pretended that I did not notice. Ethan waited until Ginger and I were midway between Grandpa, Dad, and Margaret—until we were half-pipped—and then I slowed down even more. Dad stopped, called to Ethan—not to me—to catch up. Ethan looked toward Ginger and me, then toward Grandpa and Margaret, waited another second or two, and then walked fast-forward until he caught up with Dad, Grandpa, and Margaret.

On Tuesday evening we watched a nest hatch. It was one of theirs. "Theirs" means that it was one that Margaret had moved. Like the one on the first night of our turtle walks, this one also contained a hundred and seven eggs, but this time all one hundred seven turtles emerged. "One hundred percent," Grandpa cried, and he hugged Margaret. Then he congratulated Ethan and Dad. Ginger and I stayed on the fringe because I had to hold Ginger on a short leash so that she would not start chasing the baby turtles. Grandpa did not hug or congratulate me.

We all returned to Grandpa's apartment, and Dad insisted on taking us all out to the Dairy Queen to celebrate. Margaret ate a whole Peanut Buster Parfait without once mentioning cholesterol or calories.

I was sitting at poolside, reading. After doing our turtle walk, Margaret had gone to her volunteer duties at the garden club, and Grandpa Izzy had gone to his at the public library. Ethan and I were to let ourselves into their condo and start lunch. Ethan finished his laps and came out of the water. He sat at the deep end with his legs dangling into the water. I joined him at the pool's edge and put my feet into the water, too. I noticed that he had his key on an elastic cord around his ankle, and I also noticed that he had a key chain ornament that looked like a giant molar. As the daughter of a dental hygienist, I was interested in his key chain ornament and asked him where he got it.

"From your mother," he said.

I was not prepared for his answer. "My mother?" I asked in a voice that was too loud even for the out-of-doors.

"Well, yes. Your mother works for Dr. Gershom, doesn't she?"

"As a matter of fact, she does."

"She cleaned my teeth," he said.

There is not a worse feeling in this world than the feeling that someone knows something about you that he has known for almost a whole summer and has kept to himself. Even sharing what he knows about you with others is not as bad as knowing something and not telling you he knows. All you can think about is what he was really thinking the whole time he was speaking to you or walking the beach with you or swimming laps or playing fetch with your dog Ginger. I felt as if I had been spied on. I felt as if I had been stalked.

My heart was pumping gallons of blood up to my face. I could feel my neck throb. I controlled my voice so that it would not quiver. I said, "You should have told me that. You should have told me long before now. A person with good manners would have."

Ethan said, "I didn't think it was important."

I caught my breath and asked an intermediate question, "Does your mother also know Dr. Gershom?"

"He's our family dentist."

"And Margaret? Does she also know him?"

"I told you. He is our family dentist. Grandma Draper is part of our family. Before she moved to Florida, he was her dentist, too."

"Do not adopt that tone with me, Ethan Potter."

"What tone?"

"The tone of being patient and tolerant as if the questions I am asking are dumb questions. They are not dumb questions. I need to know what you know that I do not."

"I don't know what you don't know, so how can I know what I know and you don't?"

"Now, that is a dumb question. That is really a very stupid question."

"I don't think so."

"Just tell me what you knew about my mother and me and my father before we met."

"Okay. I'll tell you what I know about you if you'll tell me what you knew about me."

"All right. You go first."

"When your mother said that she was divorcing your father and wanted to move to New York where she grew up, my grandmother set things up with Dr. Gershom."

"Margaret set what things up?"

"The job interview."

"Mother's job interview with Dr. Gershom?"

"I thought that was what we were talking about—your mother's job with Dr. Gershom."

"We are talking about what you know that I do not."

"And I am trying to tell you. Your mother told Izzy and Grandma Draper that she wanted to move to New York State, so Grandma set up a job interview with Dr. Gershom."

I had stayed in Florida with Dad while Mother had gone north to find a job and a house. No one—not Dad, not Mother, not Grandpa Izzy—no one had told me that Margaret had set up Mother's job interview with Dr. Gershom. Margaret could have. The others should have. No one seemed to think that it would matter to me where I lived. No one seemed to think that it would matter to me whether I spent my life in New York or Florida or commuting between the two.

My throat was dry. I took a deep breath of the chlorine-saturated pool air and asked, "Is there anything else you know about me that I don't know?"

Ethan shrugged. "Only that Noah was best man at Grandma and Izzy's wedding."

"The whole world knows that. I am asking you one last time. What do you know about me that I do not know you know?"

"Not much. Only that Noah never said what nice guys your dad and Izzy are."

"That is what you do not know. I was asking you what you do know." The pulse in my neck was about to break through the skin.

"I do know that you're pretty mad right now, and I think now you ought to tell me what you knew about me."

"Nothing."

"My grandmother told you nothing about me?"

"That is correct. She said nothing about you. She did not even tell me that you were coming even though she had several opportunities to do so."

Ethan then asked a strange question. "Did she tell you anything about Luke?"

"Luke what? Luke warm?"

"My brother Lucas, called Luke. Did she tell you anything about him?"

"She did not."

Ethan smiled, more to himself than to me. "Well," he said, "we Potters make an art of silence."

"Your grandmother is a Draper."

"See?" he said, grinning. "It comes to me from both sides of my family."

I did not speak to him for the rest of the day, and when he left the pool to return to the condo for lunch, I did not go with him. I thought that it would do him good to know how it felt to be the recipient rather than the giver of silence.

It was obvious that it was Margaret who had made possible my mother's leaving my father. Margaret Diamondstein, formerly Draper, helped my mother move to New York. She moved turtles from one nest to another. She moved Grandpa Izzy out of Century Village. And now, she was helping my father get permitted. By next turtle season, she will be helping him move to the beach. Margaret Diamondstein, formerly Draper, was an interfering person.

I did not need Margaret interfering with my life. I would have nothing more to do with her. That meant no more walking on the beach. That meant no more swimming and breakfast. That meant no more turtle walks.

Never again a turtle walk. Never.

I would stop and never tell her why.

Never.

I was still at the pool when Dad came to pick me up. I went back to the condo while they all went down to the beach to check on a nest. After I showered and dressed, I watched from the balcony, staying back by the wall where I could not be seen. Ginger whimpered to let me know that she wanted to be down there, but I thought that at the very least, my dog ought to stay by—and on—my side.

I wanted to leave my father's house. I wanted to go home, to autumn.

• • •

That evening as we were driving back to swinging singles, I asked my father if he knew that Margaret had set up Mother's job interview.

"I did."

"I think you could have told me."

"I didn't think it was important."

"Why does everyone think they know what is important to me? This was important. This *is* important. Do you think it is right that you should know and Ethan should know, and I should not?"

All he said was, "I didn't know that Ethan knew." I waited for Dad to say something more, to apologize, or simply tell me that I was right, but he did not. Like Ethan, my father has a strong taste for silence. Mother always said, "Your father is not a communicator." She made that statement more than once. Sometimes more than once a day. I was glad that I had made the decision not to go on any more turtle walks and not to communicate with anyone about my decision.

The following morning when Dad knocked on my door, I was still undressed. He called through the closed door, "Better hurry. We'll be late." I said nothing. He opened the door a crack and said, "Nadia? Nadia, are you all right?"

"I am not going," I said.

"What's the matter? Don't you feel well?"

"I feel fine. I have decided to stay here."

"Why?"

"It is not important."

Dad waited by the door, waited for me to explain, but I said nothing. I wanted silence to make him as miserable as it had made me. He hesitated, then came into my room, sat on the edge of the bed, and said nothing. He hovered. I struggled with silence until I could not stand it another second, so I said, "Did you know that I did a report on turtles last year?"

"Yes. I knew that."

"You never seemed very interested in turtles when I did my report."

"I guess I had other things on my mind."

The pulse in my ears was so strong, I hardly heard him. "I guess it took an invitation from Margaret to get you interested."

"Partly that and partly that I had the time."

"Your child custody time," I said. Dad let out a long sigh and looked so embarrassed that I almost did not say what I was about to say, but I did. "I have decided not to spend your child custody time on turtle walks with Margaret and her grandson. Not today. Not tomorrow. Not ever. If you want to take turtle walks, you go ahead and take turtle walks. You can get permitted without me. All you need are turtles and Margaret." I had not only broken my silence, I was almost screaming.

Dad looked at his watch. If there is one thing I really detest, it is having someone look at his watch as he is talking to me. It says to me that time spent elsewhere is more important than time spent talking to me. "I have an appointment at the office in an hour." He glanced at his watch again.

"I am sure it is an important appointment," I said.

"Yes, it is," he replied.

Dad was so preoccupied with time that he did not even notice the sarcasm in my voice.

"Let me call Margaret to let her know we won't be there."

"You can go," I said. "You go. I would not want you to miss a turtle walk for my sake. It might interfere with your getting permitted."

"There's no way I can make it up there and back in time for my appointment."

"Are you trying to tell me that I have kept you from your turtle walk?"

"Well, no. But, yes." He looked confused. "What I meant to say is that, yes, this conversation has kept me from going on a turtle walk, but no, that is not what I am trying to tell you. You know that if it had not been for your unwillingness to go, I would have."

He glanced at his watch again. "Let me call Margaret. Then we'll have time for breakfast, and we'll talk about it." He started out the door, turned back and said, "I won't tell her why you're not coming."

"Tell her. I do not care. She knows every other thing about me. Tell her," I said. "And do not count on me for breakfast. I do not want any." I turned my back to him and my face to the pillow.

The telephone rang in the middle of the morning. I let the recorder get it. It was Margaret, telling me that she would come pick me up if I would call. I did not. Instead, I took Ginger for a walk around the golf course that borders swinging singles. When we returned, I saw that there was a message on the machine. I played it. It was Grandpa Izzy asking me to please call. I erased the message. I sat out by the pool for a while and read, came back to the apartment for lunch, and that is when I ate the breakfast cereal that my dad had put out on the counter in the kitchen. He called while I was eating. I did not pick the phone up then either.

After lunch, I took Ginger for another walk, called the airline to see how much it would cost if I changed my ticket to go home early. Thirty-five dollars. I watched three talk shows on television. One was about teenagers whose mothers flirt with their boyfriends. They were pathetic. Another was about men who said they lost their jobs because they refused to cut off their ponytails. They were pathetic. The third was about people who pierce weird body parts. One girl had a silver nail through her bellybutton, and another one had a diamond stud put in her tongue. One exposed her bellybutton, and the other stuck out her tongue. They were disgusting. The phone rang twice. It was my dad again, sounding worried that I was not answering. Then it was Margaret again, saying that she hoped we would come over since another nest was due to hatch.

I erased all the messages.

Not answering the phone but hearing what people on the other end were saying was a little bit like spying. I enjoyed it.

Dad walked into the apartment looking frazzled. He was looking very much like the unstrung self who had picked me up from the airport. "Where were you?" he demanded. "I have been calling every twenty minutes."

"I noticed," I said. When he asked me why I had not returned his calls, I said that I did not think they were important.

"I'm taking tomorrow off," he said.

"What are you going to do?" I asked. "Hover?"

"What do you mean?"

"Nothing." *Nothing* is a mean answer, but sometimes nothing works. Sometimes nothing else does.

"I thought we might go up to Disney World. You used to like Epcot."

"What will I do with Ginger?" I asked.

"Well, let me find out what accommodations they have for dogs . . ."

Just then the phone rang. Dad picked it up. I could tell by the way he was speaking that it was Grandpa Izzy asking if he would be coming over for the evening's turtle walk. When he hung up, Dad asked me if I would like to invite Ethan to come to Disney World with us. I could not believe he was asking me that question. I just stared at him.

"Well," he said, "he seemed to enjoy *The Phantom of the Opera* so much, I thought he might enjoy . . ." I continued to stare at my father and say nothing. He cleared his throat. "If you don't like the idea of asking Ethan, would you like to ask one of your friends from the old neighborhood?" He was practically pleading with me to ask some-one. Without turtles my father did not know what to do with me.

Even though Disney World was only a two hours' drive from his apartment, Dad had decided that it might be more fun if we stayed overnight at one of Disney's theme hotels. He called and got us reservations, and we went to our rooms to pack our over-night bags.

That evening a northeaster hit the coast. The winds were thirty-five miles an hour with gales up to fifty. There was coastal flooding, which meant that the low lying highways and many side roads and ramps would be closed. That meant that the interstates that were normally bumper to bumper but moving would be bumper to bumper and not moving. Before we went to bed, Dad suggested that we avoid the rush hour by starting out late in the morning instead of early.

The phone rang at midnight. Dad called in to me and said that I should pick up the phone. It was Grandpa Izzy.

"It's an emergency," he said, pleading. "Our hatchlings will be swept ashore by the winds. We have to harvest them early tomorrow before daylight. Before the birds get them. Margaret and I think you ought to drive up here now so that we can get an early start. Traffic will be impossible in the morning."

Grandpa was so sincere, so concerned about the turtles, so convinced that we would answer his 911 that it was obvious Dad had never told him that I had canceled all future turtle walks. I waited to see how Dad would turn him down. Dad did his best thing; he remained silent.

Grandpa said, "Nadia, are you there? Are you on the line, darling?"

"I am here, Grandpa . . ."

"You know what will happen if we don't gather them up. Can't you come?"

"Dad and I had plans . . ."

"What plans, darling? You don't want the baby turtles to be blown ashore and die, do you? These are babies, Nadia. They need help."

"Dad and I were going to Epcot . . ."

"Why do you want to go there to see Mr. Walter Disney's Version of the World when you can see Mother Nature's real thing?" I had to smile. Grandpa Izzy always called Disney World *Mr. Walter Disney's Version of the World*. Then he said, "Margaret and I need your help, Nadia. So do the turtles. Sometimes one species has to help another get settled." Grandpa was apologizing for not telling me about Margaret's meddling. I did not know what to say.

Dad finally spoke up, "Let Mother Nature worry about the turtles. They can take care of themselves."

But I knew that they could not. I said, "Let me talk to Dad, Grandpa. I will call you back."

After I hung up, I went into the living room. Dad was in his pajamas. Striped. I had never seen Dad sitting in the living room in striped pajamas. He said, "Don't worry about the turtles, Nadia."

I explained, "The turtles will be easy to spot–so out of place, washed up on shore. The birds will eat them."

"They couldn't possibly eat them all."

"Those that do not get eaten will be lost."

"But, surely, the tide will come back and carry the seaweed–and the turtles along with it–back out." He smiled again. "What comes ashore always washes back out. That's not a philosophical statement, Nadia. It's a fact."

"They will be lost at sea."

"Lost at sea? The sea is their home."

"They will be lost at sea," I repeated.

"Nadia," Dad said, "how can that happen?"

"You have to understand turtles to understand how that will happen."

"I don't think I do."

"I told Grandpa I would talk to you."

My father sat on the sofa, looking out of place in his striped pajamas. He nodded, a slow, thoughtful nod, and I knew that he would pay close attention, and I knew that I could explain it all.

"It all starts," I said, "the minute the new hatchlings scamper over the sand toward the light of the horizon. Once they reach the water, they begin a swimming frenzy. They do not eat. They just swim and swim until they reach the Sargasso Sea. That is when they stop, and that is when Mother Nature turns off the swimming-frenzy switch and turns on a graze-and-grow switch. For the next five to ten years, they will stay in the Sargasso Sea, feeding off the small sea animals that live in the floating mats of sargasso grass. Tonight when the wind blows that seaweed ashore, there will be a lot of immature turtles in it–swept along with the sea grass they have called home."

I paused in my narrative. I focused hard on Dad, and he focused hard on me. "Are you with me?" I asked. My father nodded, so I continued. "Here is the tragic part. Even if the tide does wash them back into the water, they will not be able to get home because once the swimming-frenzy switch is turned off, it is turned off forever. Turtles do not have an emergency power pack or a safety switch to turn it on. So, there they are, once again at the water's edge, but this time they are without a mechanism for swimming east. And that is why they will be lost at sea. They will want to graze. They will have an appetite, but they will not be where they can satisfy it, and they will not know how to get there because they cannot turn back their internal clock. They will not find home. They will not find food. They will starve and grow weak and be eaten."

My father did not once look at his watch or the clock on the table by the sofa. His listen-and-learn switch had been turned on, and his own internal clock was ticking. I studied my father, sitting on the pale gray living room sofa in his blue striped pajamas. The storm in our private lives had picked him up and put him out of place. Me, too. I, too, had been picked up from one place and set down in another. I, too, had been stranded. We both needed help resettling.

"When Grandpa says that we must harvest the turtles, he means that we must gather them up and save them in buckets. Then we take them to Marineland. When the seas calm down, they will be taken fifty miles offshore and placed in the Sargasso Sea."

Dad smiled. "They need a lift."

Ginger rubbed herself against my legs. I stroked her back. "Yes," I said, "they do."

Without another word, we returned to our rooms, Dad and I. We got dressed. When we ran out to the car, the rain was coming down in sheets, and the wind was blowing so hard that umbrellas were useless. I held the back door open for Ginger, and she hopped in. Dad and I got pretty wet just from that short run to the car, and Ginger sat on the back seat, panting and smelling like the great wet dog she was.

The rain battered the car, and the wipers danced back and forth, never really clearing the windshield. There were only a few cars on the road. We didn't pass any of them not only because it was dangerous to do so but also because we welcomed their red tail lights as a guide. Cars coming the other way made spray that splashed over the hood. Dad's hands were clenched on the steering wheel.

These northeasters dump rain in squalls that last for miles, and then they let up briefly. During one of the few lulls in the storm, Dad leaned back slightly and asked, "What do the turtles do after they've finished their five to ten years in the Sargasso Sea?"

"They go to the Azores and become bottom feeders for a few years."

"And then?"

"And then they grow up. When they are about twenty-five, they mate. The females come ashore and lay their eggs—on the same shore where they were born—and immediately return to the sea, not coming ashore again for two or maybe three years when they are again ready to lay eggs. The males never return to shore."

Dad said, "You've left something out, Nadia. They are ten when they leave the Sargasso Sea, and they are twenty-five when they mate and lay eggs. What happens during the fifteen years between leaving the Azores and mating?"

Realization hit me. I laughed out loud. We were riding into a squall again, and Dad was concentrating so hard on driving that I was not sure he was even waiting for my answer. "What is it?" he asked.

"Another switch," I said.

He took his eyes off the road long enough to demand, "Tell me, what do they do?"

"In the years between leaving their second home and their return to their native beaches, they commute. Year after year, all up and down the Atlantic, turtles swim north in the summer and south in the winter. Did you already know that?"

"I didn't know for sure, but I had my suspicions."

I had to smile. "And did you have your suspicions about me?"

"For a while," he said. Then he took his eyes off the road long enough to return my smile. "But not now."

"Of course," I said, "I will be doing the same but opposite. I will commute north in the winter and south in the summer."

"Yep," he said. "And there will be times when you or I will need a lift between switches."

"Yes," I replied, "there will be times."

The Moorchild

Eloise McGraw

—•⟡ NEWBERY HONOR, 1997 ⟡•—

RAISED AMONG THE MOORFOLK CLAN, YOUNG MOQL'S LIFE IS CHANGED FOREVER WHEN THE SECRET OF HER PARENTAGE IS DISCOVERED, REVEALING HER TO BE HALF HUMAN.

It was Old Bess, the Wise Woman of the village, who first suspected that the baby at her daughter's house was a changeling.

For a time she held her peace. Many babies were ill-favored, she told herself. Many babies cried with what seemed fury against the world—though this little Saaski had not done so as a newborn. It even seemed to Old Bess that the child had not looked quite like this for its first few months, but somehow she could never quite remember. Likely the babe just had a worse-than-usual colic. No doubt her skin, dark as a gypsy tinker's so far, would lighten so as to look more fitting with that fluff of pale hair—or the hair might darken. It was even possible that the strange, shifting color of her eyes would settle down in good time. The parents both had blue eyes—Anwara's sky blue like Old Bess's own, big Yanno the black-smith's a deeper shade. The child's were cloud gray, or moss green, even a startling lilac—never blue.

They were oddly shaped eyes—set at a slant, wide and shiny, with scarcely a glimpse of white around the iris. Old Bess, strongly reminded of the eyes of squirrels, shook off the thought. Plenty of babies looked like their great-aunts, or their third cousins, or some forebear nobody remembered, she told herself, and kept her lips closed and her face shut to the rest of the village, and her fears to herself.

She was by nature a close-tongued woman, solitary in her ways, who kept her own counsel until it was asked for—sometimes even then. Queerer still, to the minds of the villagers, she chose not to live with her daughter or kin like other widow-women, but all by herself, in the little hut where the old monk died, at the far edge of the scatter of houses where the street dwindled into a path over the moor. A mighty odd one, the others thought her. *Contrarious!* Some even said, behind their hands, *witch.* But she knew all about herbs and how to cure anything from a sore throat to a broken bone. So they put up with her.

Old Bess did not care to set them wondering—and gossiping—about her suspicions of little Saaski. Indeed, she wanted fiercely to be wrong. But she had never before seen a pair of eyes that seldom seemed the same color twice.

Anwara would admit no flaw in her precious infant. Seven years of marriage had brought her and Yanno only stillbirths. Now at last she had a child alive and healthy, like the other village wives, and would no longer feel an outsider or, worst of all, be classed with Helsa, who was barren. Helsa, wife of Alun, the only man in the village to own three cows, was not only childless but past the age of childbearing. Everyone pitied her, but it was hard to like her; her tongue was always wagging about one or another of her neighbors.

Anwara doted on the baby, and until the onset of the child's strange, persistent tantrums, had bloomed with joy. By now the bloom had faded, but still she glared down anyone who gave her

Saaski a puzzled look. She comforted and rocked. She patiently bore the screaming, though she grew thin and short-tempered as the weeks passed and little Saaski grew stronger and more active and even harder to control. Yanno was not so patient.

"Can't you keep the babe from squalling, wife! What ails it, screamin' like a boggarflook!?"

"She's got the colic, is all! Sit you down and eat your dinner and leave Saaski to them that knows more about it."

"I know that's never colic, not to go on this long. My brother's first one had colic. But it came and went, like. And the babe got over it by and by."

"So will Saaski get over it, won't you, little one? Mumma's sweetling, mumma's poppet . . . sh, shh . . ." Bending over the basketlike bed, Anwara narrowly escaped a clout from a flailing small fist. The racket grew louder, if anything.

Yanno watched and shook his head. "She'll be out of that truckle bed soon, and strong as my old ram. Look at her kick, there, will you?"

"Leave off staring at her. It frets her!"

"It's *me* that frets her," Yanno muttered, continuing to stare through narrowed eyes at his raging offspring, who glared straight back at him. Slowly he backed away. The child's scream abated slightly. "You see that?" he shouted. "It's me she can't abide! Her own da'!"

"Oh, sit you down and eat, husband! I tell you it's colic."

"Then dose her with valerian or some such! But shut her up!"

Anwara had tried valerian yesterday. Near to tears, she made a tea of St. John's wort, only to have it knocked out of the spoon and into her face while Saaski shrieked and kicked with redoubled fury. At her wits' end, Anwara tried a spoonful of honey, though it was said to be bad for little ones. At once silence settled like balm over the little house, and after a few minutes Saaski slept.

Anwara, weak-kneed with relief, snatched up her shawl and ran up the single grassy street in the bright spring afternoon to tell Old

Bess she had found the cure. Yanno sat down at last to his porridge, but he kept an uneasy eye on the truckle bed. It was plain they must never run short of honey. Best watch for another wild bee swarm, he told himself, and braid another straw skep to bring it home to. Plenty of room for three hives, out beyond the garden.

Old Bess listened to Anwara's tale of triumph, noting with sinking heart the baby's telltale rejection of St. John's wort and love of sweets. But she spoke only to encourage her daughter. "No, no, my love, a spoonful of honey will not harm Saaski; no doubt it soothes her throat. Many little ones like honey." She did not add that very few turned scarlet with fury (or terror?) when their fathers came near them.

Instead, she slid a few sidewise questions here and there into Anwara's overexcited chatter, and got the answers she dreaded. Yes, Yanno had been standing quite close to the baby; yes, wearing his belt with the iron buckle—"like every other day, Mother, what a question." And yes, the saltbox was full; the salter had come through only yesterday. Was she needing a handful?

When Anwara had gone her way—heading for the village well, where she could be sure of finding a few neighbors to share her good news—Old Bess sat at a long, grim time in thought.

The baby's birth had been normal—she had overseen it herself. And the child had been placid and easy to care for—until around about its christening day. This, as Old Bess had known uneasily at the time, had been too long delayed. Father Bosa, who lived in the town several leagues away across the moor, prevented first by illness then by a late snowstorm, had not visited the village until after the first lambs dropped. Precisely when this "colic" had first appeared, Old Bess could not say. But neither she nor any other witness would forget that christening, with the babe squirming like an eel in the priest's arms and screaming fit to deafen them all. The holy water went every which way, but whether a single drop fell on the baby's head, only God could say.

Old Bess felt sure that by that day the exchange had already been made. In the dark of some midwinter night the human child she had helped to birth had been snatched away to some hidden, heathen, elfish place, and this alien creature who hated iron and salt and holy water had been left at the blacksmith's house instead.

She had no appetite that evening for her soup and coarse flat bread, and what sleep she got was troubled with eerie dreams. At first light she put on her shawl and walked down the crooked street to the little stone house next to the smithy. Yanno had not yet gone to his forge, but was finishing his breakfast ale and chunk of bread. Anwara was bending over the hearth, setting the day's loaves on the stones to bake. She straightened in surprise, said "Well, Mother!" dusted the barley flour off her hands and came to set a stool for Old Bess.

Saaski, across the single room in her truckle bed, seemed fast asleep.

"I must talk with you," said Old Bess heavily. With a sigh she dragged off her shawl, sat down, and told them what she feared and why she feared it.

For a moment they simply gaped at her, stunned and speechless. "You're mad," Anwara whispered in a trembling voice.

Old Bess, unable to watch her daughter's stricken face, or Yanno's still one, found her glance pulled toward the truckle bed. The child had raised itself and was staring straight at her, with wide-open, tilted eyes, pure lavender. Their color changed at once to smoky green. Saaski flung herself back into the bedclothes and began to scream.

Anwara was up in an instant, running to snatch the child into her arms, glaring over its struggling, twisting body at her mother. "There now!" she cried furiously. "Just see what you've done with your wicked lies! Hush, my little one! Sh—shhh . . ." She patted and soothed and jiggled without the slightest effect, shouting over the racket, half sobbing, that it was lies, all lies, and she would hear no more of it, ever.

"Will you not fetch the honey, wife?" Yanno roared, and himself strode across to the shelf and brought her the jug and the horn spoon. Saaski shrank from him and screamed louder. He backed away, glancing at Old Bess, who shrugged.

"It is not you, Yanno. It is the iron you have about you."

"God's mercy, woman! I am the smith! I will always have iron about me!"

"Then she will always shrink from you."

Yanno dropped onto his stool again, his gaze on his daughter, whom the honey had quieted. "I cannot believe it," he muttered. "I must not. I will not."

"No, nor will any folk in their senses!" snapped Anwara. She held the baby close, turned a defiant shoulder to her mother. "I beg you will not spread this gossip in the village! Think of Guin, ever wanting to belittle Yanno, and Helsa, and that sour wife of Guthwic the potter–ah, what she would give to put me down! And besides, the talk, the talk–and they would all come here, prying, and peering in the window–"

"Daughter, I am no gossip," said Old Bess. "Or liar, either."

Anwara fell silent, but her face was hard and closed.

"Do you not want your true child back?" Old Bess pleaded. "If you would believe me–"

"I *have* my child! She is here in my arms!"

"Nay, wife, peace, peace–" Yanno waved her quiet with a big hand, and turned to Old Bess. "Supposing we did believe you–nay, Anwara, let me have my word now. Supposing it was all so. What should we do then, eh, old woman? How could we rid ourselves of the pixie, or elf-thing, or moorchild, or whatever 'tis, and get our own babe back?"

Old Bess had dreaded the question. "There are ways, I'm told." She chose the mildest. "The changeling will be gone in a blink, so they say, if it is only made to tell its age. For it may be no babe at all, but older than old."

"Then we must wait for the great news till Saaski's old enough to talk," retorted Anwara with a scornful laugh.

Yanno thought about this and raised his bushy eyebrows at Old Bess. "Aye, so far the little one speaks no word even a heathen could understand. Tell us another cure."

Old Bess took a deep breath. "I have heard—but I cannot swear it—that the Folk will come and take their creature back if—if it be thrown into a well—or onto the fire—or sorely beaten."

"Fire? Beaten?" Anwara gasped. She backed away, clutching the now silent child tighter than ever. "I, do such to the babe I bore? Whatever are you saying?"

"But that is not the babe you bore!" cried her mother. "That is not even a human child—"

Yanno's deep rumble broke in. "Enough! Let be." His gaze on Old Bess had turned somber. "You mean well, old woman. But I'll hear no more of these cures. I doubt I could so ill-treat any creature. Not when it looks so like a child."

Old Bess looked at their faces, rose, put on her shawl, and went back to her own hearth, her feet heavy and slow with her failure. She had spoken too soon, or not soon enough—she had troubled her son-in-law, set her daughter's face against her, and only hardened their defense of the baby Saaski. Now there was nothing to do but wait for time and trouble to change their minds.

While Anwara, torn between fear and fury, went brooding about her daily tasks, Saaski lay in the truckle bed uncharacteristically silent. She, too, was brooding. And she was thinking hard.

She was not much in the habit of thinking, only of howling her bitter, lonely anger at her exile from all she knew and understood—her homeland, the Folk and their paths crisscrossing the moor, her numberless kin.

She neither tried nor wished to understand the alien human life around her. Through the long days, caged in the hateful truckle bed, bored and homesick, she had done little but rage and grieve.

She cared nothing for her jailers—not the young woman who fed her the tasteless gruel and half smothered her with embraces, not the old woman who was her enemy, not the man with his fearful, threatening iron. They might live out their clumsy human lives or die tomorrow, for all of her. They might have their own babe back with her goodwill. Indeed, nothing would have pleased her more than to be gone in a blink, as the old woman said, back home to the Mound and the Moorfolk, leaving this truckle bed to its silly rightful owner.

But she had no fancy at all for these "cures." To be beaten by that great hulking man with his fists like mallets and his smell of iron was a terrifying thought. As for being thrown onto the fire—! Yanno's scruples would vanish the moment he stopped thinking of her as a child—and soon or late, with that old woman's help, he would stop. Besides, suffering his blows would serve no purpose. The Folk might whisk her away from him, but they would only cast her out a second time, changed for some different human child. And to be put twice to the trouble would annoy them. Next time they might drop her into a far worse place, to pay her out.

As for telling her age, nobody could trick her into that, for she did not know it herself—only that she was still a youngling, just old enough for the others to discover that she could not hide.

She'd left the Nursery some time before, and moved into Schooling House with the rest of the half-grown young ones of the band, to learn the work and the paths. Every twilight she joined one of the ever-shifting groups of younglings led by old Flugenlul or Nottoslom or some other mentor, raced with them out of the earthen doorway of Schooling House, across the vast, twinkling cavern known as the Gathering and up the long, twisting, twining staircase of the Mound, chattering and pushing. Silent a moment at the top, then out through the main portal behind the great boulder, and onto the moor—evening after evening, the unruly troop of them, to spread out, running and skipping, under the enormous sky. The open air, the sharp, fresh scents of bracken and heather and stone and always rain—whether past or present or on its way—seemed new each night, too exciting to allow for any settling down until they'd run the kinks out of their legs.

But then old Flugenlul would summon them from wherever they'd scattered, and make them stay on the Folk paths while they did their evening's work. Sometimes he led them down into the wood at the moor's edge to gather twigs for firewood, or along the fringes of the lake below that to cut reeds for bundling into torches. Mostly they stayed on the high moor, collecting thistle-silk for the spinners back in the Mound, and tufts of wool left here and there by the humans' browsing sheep. They found old twists of cobweb for the weavers and cord makers, wild fruits and herbs and mushrooms for the cooks, bracken and leaves and grasses to renew and sweeten the beds. Occasionally a couple of the bravest, Zmr or Tinkwa, stole away to the village and into a farmer's stable, to spend a giggling hour tangling his horse's mane or tying the cows' tails together. The braggart Els'nk boasted of venturing into the farmhouse itself, to tickle the sleeping humans with ice-cold hands, but nobody believed him. It was only the elder Folk who dared such pranks.

Some whole evenings the younglings spent watching over the tiny moon-white Folk cows with their red horns and eyes, at midnight driving them back to their hidden byre. Now and then they did no work all night, but stole old Flugenlul's bagpipes and took turns playing them, or tied his beard to his weskit button and snatched his red cap and danced just out of reach when he grabbed at them.

Before dawn they filed back through the boulder-hidden portal again and down the long stair—often mounting the handrail and spiraling down, one after the other—and back to Schooling House, ready to sleep awhile and eat something. Later an ever-curious youngling like Saaski—though that was not yet her name, in the Mound it was Moql'nkkn—a curious few like Moql might venture together out into the Gathering, the Mound's central common.

It was a vast, airy cave, the Gathering, a hollow in the rough crystalline rock that twinkled and glinted in the upper dimness as it caught the light in a million pinpoints. The light came from coldfire torches embedded in the rock walls, from scattered cookfires around which couples or groups collected and dispersed as impulse or hunger moved them, and from the greenish glow that was ever present in the Mound. There was constant flitting up and down the twisting stairway as the Moorfolk with their dark, clever faces and floating pale hair went about their erratic pursuits and whatever work was necessary to keep the band prosperous and well fed.

Among them the little knots of younglings could wander, elbows or long fingers touching, big, slanted eyes observing the life of their elders—a life freer and wilder but as haphazard as their own.

"I see your mama!" they teased each other. "There! See? That ugly one over there!"

It was a silly joke; only the youngest, fresh from the Nursery, ever stared about, saying, "Where? Where?" Moql was one who at first had stared eagerly around. But then she saw that all the others were giggling, so after a moment she giggled, too. No youngling knew its mother—only that it must have had one. Each mother cosseted and adored her baby until the Nursery took over, then she forgot it and returned to the Gathering and a different mate and the careless life of the Folk, in which a great deal of everybody's time, whether in the Mound or Outside in the humans' world, was spent in dancing, feasting, mischief, idling, and dreaming. Food gathering was a game of light-fingered skill—stealing eggs from the moorhens' nests, nuts from the squirrels' hoards, lentils and milk from the villagers and their cows. They boasted of their pranks around the cookfires; one had stripped a farmer's honeycombs, another emptied a fisherman's basket as fast as he filled it, a third had shared a shepherd's lunch. The younglings eavesdropped on the tales and could hardly wait till they were full-grown and skillful, too.

It was a life without yesterdays or tomorrows—life as it was meant to be, Moql thought then, when she knew no other. And it went on, seamlessly, until she and the other younglings had finished their nighttime learning and began to go abroad by day–to find out about dogs and iron and crosses, and humans who were not safely asleep but awake and wary. They were taught to find the paths in sunlight, to note and heed the runic signs left by the Folk on barns or gates or doorways, and to make the secret runes themselves.

Then one day they were called upon to hide–and everything ended in the wink of an eye for Moql'nkkn.

It was a sudden test and a harsh one. That morning they were not allowed to lurk behind things while an elder pointed out a Man, a Woman, a Shepherd Boy, a Cross Dog and a Silly Dog, and warned them of cats–which could always see the Folk and were to be avoided. Instead they were abruptly turned loose to go where they would, in plain sight of each other and the human world.

"But mind now, if one of Them comes along, *hide,*" warned Pit-tittiskin, who was instructing them that day. "Not while they're gawking straight at you, wait till they blink. Then you can do a shape change, or a color change, or go dimlike, or run up a tree, or just wink out–that's best, if you hold your breath till you can slip behind a rock or something. But don't let Them see, you hear? You'll endanger the Band." He strolled away, turned back casually. "If you muff it and get caught, remember about the gold."

"What if They're on our path, though?" Moql asked him, peering uneasily over her shoulder. She found this much freedom scary.

A chorus of youngling voices piped up. "Pinch 'em!" "Trip 'em!" "Pull their hair!" "Change into an adder!" "A hornet!" "A bear!"

"A *bear*?" echoed somebody, and the belligerence dissolved in laughter.

But Pittittiskin snapped, "The paths are ours! However you do it, keep Them off!" He turned away again, took a flying leap into a chestnut tree and began to tease Jinka, with whom he had paired off lately, and wind the long leaves into her silvery hair.

The younglings, left to their own devices, drifted apart, some joining playmates higher up the moor, others searching for mushrooms at the edge of the woodland. Moql found a few wild berries and wandered from bush to bush, with no heed to where she was straying until she all but fell over a big, brown, gray-faced ewe lying in the shade of a clump of bracken. The ewe stumbled to its feet with a noisy *blaa-aa-aatt* and galumphed off. Moql, equally startled, looked around to find the flock scattered about the hillside, and herself in its midst, with every woolly gray face turned her way. The shepherd—not a Boy, either, but a full-grown Man carrying a dangerous-looking crook—was striding across the flank of the hill straight toward her, with his jaw dropped and his eyes half starting from his head.

"Hide! Hide! Hide!" shrilled a voice from somewhere, but it called in the secret tongue, which the Folk understood well enough, but only made humans gawk about trying to spot the unknown bird.

Every youngling Moql could see obeyed. The dozen playing a ring game near the crest had vanished, though quite a number of crows, with a chicken or two oddly mixed in, now pecked in the same spot among the grasses. Out of the corner of her eye Moql glimpsed Tinkwa running like a red-capped lizard up an outcrop, with Zmr, already rock-colored, right behind.

With the shepherd's eye full on her, she herself dared only shrink a bit and go bluish like the shadows under the bracken, fighting off panic as she waited for him to blink. Suddenly a near-transparent shape—it was Els'nk—darted from behind a berry bush and flung a handful of dirt into the shepherd's staring eyes, and then he had to squint and rub them. Thankfully Moql gulped in her breath to wink out, held it hard, and left the flimsy shelter of the bracken to dash in invisible safety across the open space toward Els'nk's bush.

She had scarcely started when a large hand grasped the back of her hooded jacket and yanked her off her feet to dangle like a puppy held by its scruff. She gasped, realizing the trick must not have worked. Why not? She was sure to be visible now, for the jerk had shaken her held breath loose. In terror she kicked and struggled, trying to change to an eel, to a horned toad, trying to turn a fearsome bright yellow with red spots, trying desperately to hold her breath again, whether the Man was watching or not. But nothing would work while he held her. From all around came the cries of the unknown bird as the Folk shrieked for her to try what she was already trying, warned her needlessly that it was a *Man.*

Then the shepherd's dog rose among the grasses and began to bark, and the voices ceased amid a sudden clapping of wings. The crows flapped aloft, the few chickens stretched out their necks and ran helter-skelter. Moql could not see whether Els'nk was still behind the berry bush, or Zmr and Tinkwa on the outcrop. She could not see any Folk at all, twist how she would, because her captor had turned her to face him and was holding her, still by a handful of jacket, to look her over.

Fearfully she raised her eyes to meet his astonished gaze.

"A pixie, all right enough," he muttered. "Mebbe a Dark Elf. What are you, little one? Can you talk a Christian tongue?"

Moql's lips clamped shut. The dog trotted closer, barking until the man silenced it.

"Can't or won't," said the shepherd. "Be y' full grown? Shouldn't think so. Near the size of my five year old, but skinnier, no more weight to you than a kitten." He turned her this way and that, lifted her higher to study her long, arched feet. "Eh, how my little Davvy 'ud like a peek at you! But you might do 'im a mischief, so you might. There's tales of your kind." He scrutinized her a moment longer, then burst into a gleeful laugh. "So I went and caught one, sure enough! I never held with them stories. Eh, they'll call me a liar, over t'moor in my village." He paused. "Less'n I bring you back with me."

Moql squirmed desperately—she couldn't help it. The man's eyes narrowed. "By gorrikins, I think you do know what I'm sayin'." He peered at her, frowning a little. "Here, now. I mean you no harm, pixie." (Moql squirmed again, this time with annoyance. The Folk did not care to be confused with distant, possibly lowborn cousins.) "Here, we'll strike a bargain. They say your kind has got stores of gold hid all around these hills. Is it so, then?"

Moql went still. *If you muff it and get caught, remember about the gold.* "It is," she said—her voice so shaky and squeaky she could barely hear it herself.

The man said, "Eh?" and held her up to his hairy ear. She gathered her strength and shrilled *"It is!"* straight into it, so that he held her away hastily.

"Right, then! Just show me where, you see? And I'll let you go, I will."

Moql knew what to do next—but the dog, a terrible shaggy creature with bright, intent eyes, was sitting just below her, with a tongue as long as her forearm lolling out between his wicked teeth. "I'm afeard of *him*," she said.

"Ah, never you mind about Trusty, he'll do as he's bid and naught else. Here, off with you, boy, round up your stragglers!" The shepherd waved his crook, and the dog loped away as if the gesture had flung him. "Now—no tricks, little 'un—where's the treasure hid?"

"Let me loose and I'll take you there." It was worth a try.

He only laughed at her. "Think I'm a noddikins? You'd be off afore I could blink! Just tell me straight."

"Well, gold's down in the woods yonder, buried. You find the fifth tree west of the red fox's hole. Then you walk a snake's length south and find old Twilligard's sign on a fallen log—less'n the moss has covered it—then you go where it says, and—"

"Here, hold on! Where's this red fox's hole? How'll I find that?"

Moql shrugged as well as she could for one suspended in midair. "*I* know where 'tis. You'll have to hunt."

"Nay, then. You'll have to show me," the shepherd retorted. He gave her a hitch and shifted his grasp to her middle, tucking her under his arm like a parcel as he strode down toward the woods.

There wasn't any fox's hole, red or otherwise, but Moql pointed to something and he took her word for it, then they struggled along what she told him was a snake's length south, which led him through nettles and brambles straight up to a dense thicket, with not a fallen log in sight. Here he balked—to her relief, since she was sore and breathless from the jolting. He held her up again and glowered at her.

"Think me a muggins, do you? I'll go no farther. You tell me straight now, or I'll give you to me dog!"

"It's just yonder," she said hastily, pointing at random. "'Twixt the roots of that big oak. You'll have to dig."

"*You'll* dig, pixie!" He stalked over to the oak and swung her down among the ancient roots, keeping a fast hold on her jacket.

Gladly she burrowed into the soft mold of earth and last year's leaves, and in a moment twisted toward him, offering a little handful of golden coins with the dirt still clinging to them.

His eyes bulged. Slowly he took them, letting his crook fall. He bit one. "By m'faith they're real!" he whispered. "By jings, and I never believed it."

"Plenty more," Moql told him.

"Here, move aside, pixie, let me there," he said, suddenly brisk. "I can dig faster nor you."

He swept her away and fell to work. She didn't tarry to watch. One jubilant leap and she was among the branches, already leaf color. Next moment she was safe in a high crotch, hugging the mossy trunk and fading to gray green to match it—or trying to. She peered anxiously at her doubled-up legs, her hands. Yes, gray green as moss, as lichen. It was all right, she knew how, the other was some kind of mistake that would never happen again. From here and there in neighboring trees came birdlike giggles, in which she joined with relief and delight, her heart still pounding but her self-esteem swelling like a bubble. She had served that great gorm a turn, she had! Now *she* would have something to boast of!

"Clumsy youngling!" said a caustic voice from a branch above her.

The bubble burst. She looked up into Pittittiskin's disdainful countenance. "I did it right!" she protested.

"The gold trick, aye. Everything else wrong. Slow. Bad. Risky. You never winked out at all."

Before she could argue there came an outraged bellow from the foot of the tree, followed by "*Pixie!* Here, where'd you get to? Ahhh . . . that hoaxing creetur! I mighta known . . . !"

She glanced down through the leaves at the shepherd's head and burly shoulders. The gold would have turned back into leaf mold by now. She no longer relished the joke. Stonily she watched as he turned this way and that, calling her several words she'd never heard before, then stomped off up the hill to his sheep.

"Back to the Mound!" Pittittiskin ordered.

"At midday? But we barely—You mean all of us? But we'll learn, we're only beginners—"

"Nay, just you. The others are beginners. You're a blunder-head." Pittittiskin landed on her branch, seized her hand and leaped, half floating, to the ground, taking her along willy-nilly.

She wailed and tugged to free her hand. "Let me try again, I'll do better . . ."

"Give over, now!" He silenced her with a yank, headed swiftly for the nearest Folk-path. "You maybe can't. There's something amiss with you, youngling, I dunno what. We'll have to see the Prince. I suspicion you're a menace to the Band."

⇥ Permissions ⇤

*If you want to read the complete Newbery
Medal and Newbery Honor books, look for them
at your local library or bookstore:*

HITTY: HER FIRST
HUNDRED YEARS
by Rachel Field
0-027-34840-7 hc
0-689-82284-7 pbk

THE CAT WHO WENT
TO HEAVEN
by Elizabeth Coatsworth
0-027-19710-7 hc
0-689-71433-5 pbk

CALICO BUSH
by Rachel Field
0-027-34610-2 hc
0-689-82285-5 pbk

CADDIE WOODLAWN
by Carol Ryrie Brink
0-027-13670-1 hc
0-689-71370-3 pbk

MISTY OF CHINCOTEAGUE
by Marguerite Henry
0-027-43622-5 hc
0-689-71492-0 pbk

THE COURAGE OF
SARAH NOBLE
by Alice Dalgliesh
0-684-18830-9 hc
0-689-71540-4 pbk

FROM THE MIXED-UP
FILES OF MRS. BASIL E.
FRANKWEILER
by E. L. Konigsburg
0-689-20586-4 hc
0-689-71181-6 pbk

JENNIFER, HECATE,
MACBETH, WILLIAM
MCKINLEY, AND ME,
ELIZABETH
by E. L. Konigsburg
0-689-30007-7 hc

THE HEADLESS CUPID
by Zilpha Keatley Snyder
0-689-20687-9 hc

THE TOMBS OF ATUAN
by Ursula K. Le Guin
0-689-31684-4 hc

A GATHERING OF DAYS: A
NEW ENGLAND GIRL'S
JOURNAL, 1830–32
by Joan W. Blos
0-684-16340-3 hc
0-689-71419-X pbk

DICEY'S SONG
by Cynthia Voigt
0-689-30944-9 hc

YOLONDA'S GENIUS
by Carol Fenner
0-689-80011-0 hc
0-689-81327-9 pbk

THE VIEW FROM SATURDAY
by E. L. Konigsburg
0-689-80993-X hc
0-689-81721-5 pbk

THE MOORCHILD
by Eloise McGraw
0-689-80654-X hc
0-689-82033-X pbk